LOST AND ALONE

When we got home I invited Chad into my room to sit together with me in my bean chair while we played checkers. He used to love that, but tonight he pulled away, and looking me straight in the eyes in his honest innocent little way, he said, "You're not Jay anymore . . . You don't look like Jay . . . You don't smell like Jay . . . You don't act like *Jay.*" He stared at me intently for a minute and then kind of whimpered, "Who are you?"

Sweet little Chaddy, that was so unlike him, but in his childlike purity and incorruption he knows . . . Chaddy alone knows . . . that I no longer control my own destiny, own my own body, I am no longer captain of my ship, no longer master of my soul.

JAY'S JOURNAL

ANONYMOUS

Edited by
Dr. Beatrice Sparks

POCKET BOOKS
New York   London   Toronto   Sydney   Tokyo   Singapore

Times, places, names and some details have been changed to protect the privacy and identity of Jay's family members and friends.

POCKET BOOKS, a division of Simon & Schuster Inc.
1230 Avenue of the Americas, New York, NY 10020

Copyright © 1979 by Beatrice Sparks
Cover art copyright © 1989 Mort Engel Studio

Published by arrangement with the author

ISBN: 0-671-73559-4

First Pocket Books printing June 1989

10

POCKET and colophon are registered trademarks of Simon & Schuster Inc.

Printed in the U.S.A.

Dedicated to every kid who might need to do some soul-searching in his or her own life, to ask himself or herself: Can *I* handle things if I continue to pursue my present course?

INTRODUCTION

At 7 A.M. January 3, 1978 a very distressed mother phoned. She said she had read an article about how I had prepared *Go Ask Alice* from an existing diary, and *Voices*, not then released, from personal interviews; how I hoped both books would help educate young people as to the problems and pressures and weaknesses of their peers, and make it easier for them to consider alternatives and make wise decisions in their own lives.

The lady said her son, Jay, had kept a journal—a seminary book—and many papers and letters, which she felt could also be of benefit to both kids and parents looking for answers and ways out.

Jay, 16½ years old, had been into witchcraft, how deeply neither his mother nor his father had ever suspected, until after Jay put his father's pistol against his right temple and pulled the trigger.

As Jay's mother and I plowed through the many containers of favorite footballs, basketballs, tennis rackets, trophies, diplomas, awards, letters, notes, books, etc., that she had not been able to part with, she remained calm and helpful. Only when she unfolded Jay's worn, stained "grub jacket" at the bottom of the last box did she cry; telling me how she had put the leather patches on the elbows after his motorbike had gone out of control and spilled down the slope and into a tree, how she had replaced the front pocket with an emblem he had picked up on a trip to Las Vegas, how he had stained the front lapel and shoulder helping his dad bring a deer down on a pole slung over both their shoulders, how he had made the long slash on the right arm when he had rescued their cat, Hamlet, from the top of a 200-foot tree, how the two stars over the left breast represented his "eternal and forever" buddies, Dell and Brad.

From the corner of the lining she patiently pulled out a half-eaten, linty M&M and holding it, as reverently as though it were the Sacrament, she whispered almost to herself, *"Jay always thought he could handle anything, everything!"*

Jay was an exceptionally intelligent and articulate boy, with an I.Q. of 149+. In his journal, he often worried that his best friends weren't able to handle things the way he could because of his detached, intellectual approach. He analyzed, composed lists, fought against giving in. But he was sometimes relieved when he didn't *have* to handle things—drugs, alcohol, the occult, or even sex.

Jay's journal became his intimate confidante. In it, he felt free to express his confusions, his hopes, and his fears.

Hoping to fill in sketchy gaps in Jay's journal I interviewed many of his friends and teachers. As a whole they said he was a "mostly just like everybody else" boy. Three kids who had been into the occult with him seemed more skittish. As long as we were talking about school, dating, family, drugs, hobbies, or sports, they were relaxed and friendly, but when I tried to question them about witchcraft they changed, became frightened, secretive, withdrawn. Through bits and pieces I gathered that they were under some strange kind of "sacrifice my own life or have it taken from me" type of programming. They sincerely seemed to fear that I could bring harm to myself or my own kids if more information were divulged to me. Their obvious and abject terror was contagiously and hauntingly real. I wanted out and I wasn't even in!

Jay's mother's voice returns, *"Jay always thought he could handle anything, everything!"*

That dirge, much more repeated than most people imagine, mixes with the lonely cry of every frightened little girl I ever worked with or talked to who found herself pregnant: "I didn't think it could happen to me!"

The voice of every kid hooked on drugs, alcohol, or the occult joins the sad chorus, "Not me! I didn't think it could ever happen to me. I WAS SURE I COULD HANDLE IT!"

BEATRICE SPARKS

July 2

For two weeks now my Sunday school teacher and my scout master and everybody else have been on my ass to keep a journal. It's the biggie now! The new 'everybody's got to do it' thing! Mom bought me this one and left it on my bed when the hassle first began. I know she expected me to be 'appreciative' about something I didn't even want and more especially don't want to do! But like usual, *what I want* is not important, it's what I'm *supposed to do* that counts! The old man is always moaning about how he works his tail off for us, and how . . . Oh, Judas, this isn't what you're supposed to put in a journal. You're supposed to put only good things that your kids and grandkids and all of posterity can read. Man, I don't want any kids if they're going to turn out, burn out, anything like me; sad, rebellious, angry, searching . . . searching . . . searching, and for what? I'm going on fifteen years old and no answers yet have ever really satisfied me. I want more . . . and more . . . and more! But more what? What in the hell do I *really* want out of life? That's one of the things this dumb-ass journal is supposed to help me find out, but at this rate it's just going to get me into more rocking trouble than I'm already in, if that's possible. If the kids read it they'll go tattling to mom and dad, and if *they* read it all hell will break loose and I'll get grounded for completely through the millennium. Crap, what kind of a monster have I started here?

I don't want anybody to know what a rotten bastard

screw-up I am, and always have been, probably from the beginning of time and before. I'm trying to keep it from myself even! . . . yet here I am putting it all down in incriminating black and white . . . Judas, boredom is a drag, drag, drag. Writing might be good therapy for me in a way, though. Indeed, a means of getting hostile things out of my system. It seems like I'm eternally out of sync . . . kind of like I always want to scream 'black' when somebody says 'white,' or whatever is, to quote the old man, 'argumentative, inappropriate and revolutionary.'

> He wanted in
> I wanted out
> He had a smile
> I had a pout
> I need someone to understand
> God, how I need a helping hand.

Man, if people are going to keep a journal they should do it when they're little, when all the good things happen, before life starts kicking you in the ass and in the head and every other place. When I was little before I even knew how to write was the only time things happened that were worth writing about. No, I remember going to Disneyland with the family when I was bigger, and going on fishing trips and on the deer hunts with my mom's brothers and sisters and my dad's relatives. We would all meet up at Big Pines and have a campground where the kids ran like wild Indians through the brush and streams and groves while the dads and big boys went up into the very tops of the mountains. Judas, it was exciting when they brought their deer down across their backs or on the tote-goat.

The girls would gag and shudder while they cut the heads off and skinned the things and we guys would rub salt into the pelts with rocks and have the greatest times ever.

But then somehow I got into seventh grade and started smoking shit and stuff and I don't know, I guess it really was in seventh grade when I starting getting off the track. Man, it all seems so strange now, when I was in first and second and third grade I was so square and religious and everything. I'd looked forward to being a deacon for as long as I can remember—I really wanted to pass the Sacrament! And I'd been saving my money to go on a mission since I first knew what money was.

I was so sincere then, and I tried so hard to conform. At least a part of me did. What happened to that sweet little kid? Whatever—ever happened to that nice little boy that I will never know again? I feel sad, like someone has died, maybe a part of me has . . . the good part.

January 7

Hi, you dumb bastard old journal:

I haven't written in you for six months, haven't even thought about you in fact, until tonight when I'm so bored I'm about to fall out of my tree. Judas, when I remembered I had hid you up in the attic, under the insulation by the crawl hole in my bedroom, it was like rediscovering an old friend. How's that for being lonely? Being grounded is really the shits. I've been imprisoned for a week and I've read and studied and drawn till I'm about to go stir crazy, all because I punched Kendall out for getting in my room and messing up my stuff. I just threw him out in the hall after I'd already told him a hundred million times to bug off. How in hell was I supposed to know he'd land the wrong way and break his arm?

The saddest thing is that everybody acts like I broke it on purpose. They should all know me well enough to know I wouldn't . . . I couldn't . . . do anything like that. They forget it was me that jumped in after him when he fell into the Snake River in Yellowstone Park; and me that packed him down the mountain when he ran through the patch of poison ivy and got it in his eyes and stuff; and me that always fixes his bicycle when the chain comes off or it has a flat or . . . Oh, God, he's such a neat little guy and I feel *soooooooooo* bad inside. I wish like everything it was my arm that was busted! I'd even sit right here and break both my arms if I thought that would help any. I really would!

I'm sorry . . . *sorry* . . . SORRY AS HELL! Man, I'm sorry! I don't know why I can't tell any of them that though. It's like I speak Chinese and they all speak Russian or some screw-up thing. They don't understand! They don't think I 'care,' I 'hurt,' or I 'have feelings.' It just seems like I'm always wrong, always 'selfish,' always 'self-centered,' and everything else that's negative and destructive. Oh dear God, I don't want to be all these things. Please somebody help me not to be them. I want to be loved and treated special and stuff like the little kids are. Will it ever be that way again? *Can* it ever again be for me like it was when I was little?

January 14

I had an I.Q. test in school today and it's 149+. Man, that makes me so proud! A genius! Me a genius! Well, almost. I found out by accident when I heard the teacher talking to the guy who gives the tests. I was walking down the hall being loud, trying to get a little attention for my old mismatched self, hitting guys and pushing girls, saying weird, gross things, just being old goofy loony me, maybe even more obnoxious than usual because Brad and Dell were both out with the flu. In a way I'm kind of glad Brad and Dell weren't with me when I found out about my I.Q. because . . . well, it's hard to be different. I checked under Intelligence Quotient in the library and only 7 percent of privileged kids are high as me. That's scary. I'm afraid of being different. It's hard enough to exist when you feel mostly like everybody else. Nobody wants to be different, even good different. I want to be like Brad and Dell! We pretend we're the Three Nephites. We three against the world! Out to avenge all wrongs! Since we've been in kindergarten we've been best friends, more than friends . . . buddies . . . brothers. . . . One time we were talking seriously and decided we must have been friends in heaven before we came to this world. I can't imagine heaven being heaven without those two guys. I really can't. I know that sounds dumb-assed and hair-brained, very me-like, but I'm not really a *whole* person without them. I'm beginning to sound like my Sunday school teacher. . . . Crap on crap I don't need that!

I guess actually this high I.Q. thing is a big responsibility. I really am going to try to live up to it. I'm going to improve my vocabulary and try to be more colorful and picturesque in my speech. I think next fall I'll try to get on the debating team. It's kind of a Mickey

Mouse thing in ninth grade but at least it will prepare me for high school.

January 16

Mrs. Stewart put Debbie Dale next to me in English. I can't believe how beautiful she is! She's prettier than Charlie's Angels or anybody. Man she brings out in me all the drives known to mankind. I wish I knew how to talk to her but I just sound stupid. I tried to show her how smart I was and I came off sounding like a retard. Man, life can be soooo heavy! Debbie smells good!

Debbie Dale . . . DEBBIE DALE . . . *DEBBIE DALE!*

January 17

Today I bought Debbie a coke from the machine in the hall by the gym and wouldn't you just know the whole damn thing would squirt up all over her face. She went running off crying, and poor old dumb clod me, I just stood there. . . . The other guys were laughing so I started laughing, but I really wanted to cry.

January 18

Last night I dreamed I got it on with Debbie, but our relationship can't be that way.

> Love and respect are one.
> In the sun
> That shines in Debbie's corn silk hair
> And in her eyes of sky blue mists
> And lips that must be kissed.

I'm going to be late for school but who cares if I ever go again? Brad and Dell both told me 'for my own good' that Deb 'has been around.' Shit, crap, hell, don't they think I know that? In seventh and eighth grade everybody knew she was going with Mark Vrooder and his sleazy bunch, but she's changed.

> She's changed! I know she's changed!
> God made the beauties of the earth
> Still there was dearth
> Till he made Debbie Dale.

February 15

For once things are neat at home! I'm fifteen! Dad gave me a job in his pharmacy as a birthday present and I get to take the tote-goat to work.

Debbie went with her parents to Phoenix so Brad and Dell and me all got stoned to celebrate. We went up the canyon on our bikes with our bedrolls and our goodies and man! man! man What a trip! I had two packs of beer. Brad had, I don't know how many roaches, and Dell had some pills he'd ripped out of his mom's bottle.

I can see how Debbie used to use. If I didn't know better I'd never come down myself. I was just lying there spaced out in all that beauty of mountains and streams and trees, watching a big old hawk and really thinking I could do anything he could do, if I wanted to, and better! Man, it was neat.

I would like to stay stoned all the time, it scares me it's so good! I would like to stay stoned every minute of every day for the rest of my life! Honestly I would . . . at least a part of me would. The other part of me is excited about working in dad's store. I've always looked forward to that; sometimes I still think I'll be a pharmacist and we'll have a chain of stores. That's sort of what dad and grandpa want. I guess it's what I want too. Dad and grandpa both make lots of money in their stores and so does Uncle Burton. We'll see . . .

February 16

Debbie's home! I couldn't have stood it much longer without her! The reality of the situation is that I'm getting awfully attached to her and it's making me feel good. 'We've got something goin'!'

The energy that flows between us isn't all hyperactive. Most of it is gentle and sweet and beautiful. We have a relationship. When I am old, old, old like my dad I will still love Debbie! I'll be true to her, worship her, gear my life to hers. I don't even want to go to sleep because then I waste time not thinking about her.

February 20

Oh Debbie . . . Debbie . . . Debbie. You make me feel like a real person. Someone important and worthwhile. Sometimes I'm embarrassed because you're such a dumb-assed little blond with not so good grammar but what you do for my ego is something else again! You hang on me in the halls like we're glued together or something and instead of that being embarrassing it's more than macho . . . even with my trying to improve my vocabulary, there are no words for it. You think I'm so smart and . . . Oh Debbie I adore you! I don't think I could live without you. I really don't. I'll get straight A's for you this semester. I'll be the big jock on campus. I'll make you *more proud* of me. I tried to phone you—but you weren't home.

Life is so dull
So worthless and so small
Until you call.
Then rays of sunshine fill my soul—and I am whole.

Mom, dad, it doesn't matter that you were both Phi Beta Kappa, or that intelligence, for you, comes just under God and family. Debbie is my God . . . well, maybe not my God but just under him!

March 1

I'm grounded again. That's almost the story of my life. I wish they'd just beat me and get it over with. Parents are so sadistic. I know I shouldn't have sneaked out to see Debbie after I'd already been grounded for two days for staying out too late with her. But I had to see her. I just had to! Now that we're getting it on we're like one person. Being away from her is like not breathing. I really do, I miss her as much as air. I would even give up Brad and Dell for her. Thank God they didn't make me do that! They almost did though.

Judas, it was awful, dad meeting me at the door, his face like an iron mask, and mom's tears like icicles streaming down her cheeks. Oh crap I hate them and their heavy handedness so much! But a part of me knows they're trying to protect me too! But from Debbie? Why can't they understand her? They think she's too 'aware,' too 'worldly' for me. Everybody in this dinky town knows everything about everybody else, about their past, present and forever. Once somebody has slipped no one will ever give them a chance again, have faith in them, think they're any good. Well, I won't be that way! These smug little people in their smug little holes can keep their heads up their asses—but they can't make me do it! I'm me! Me! Me! I won't be like them . . . them . . . them!

Oh Mom—you're such a fat gross-out loser!

What do you know about love, fat hog? Are your feelings more holy than mine? Am I exempt from the knowledge of love until I become 'of age'? Do I automatically become human enough to love when I start loving you and seeing things your way? If that is the case then it may be a very long time until I am 'human' in your eyes.

(I love!)

I just read what I wrote and I'm sorry.

TO MY PARENTS

You love me
So you think this gives you rights
To mold my life like yours
But this can never be.
I must be free
I must be me!
I know I'll make mistakes
And whimper in my sleep
For all things you as parents represent—and yet
I'm not your pet.
You cannot teach me tricks—to come at your
    command
Or always lead me by the paw or hand.
To win or fail

I alone must blaze my sometimes lonely, sometimes hurting trail.

IT'S THREE A.M.

God, why are the blackened wasteful nights so long?
Why do the sunny happy days pass by so fast and
   sweet?
When Debbie sits beside my feet?
Why must my teardrops wet the pillow of my bed.
For all the unkind things I've said.
I do not want to hurt my loved ones so
How can I change?
That, only you, dear God, can know.

FIVE A.M.

Night . . . endless is thy name.

I'm like a drowning person. All the stops in the computers of my mind have fallen out and everything I've ever learned or read or heard is spilling out over each other. I'm trying to see things like others see them. I know Debbie controls me completely but she was hurt so much by the crumbs she used to go with. They *used* her! She was young and innocent and believing, and she really is trying to get off drugs. She is! I know she is! My heart tells me she is! My guts tell me she is! Why won't anyone believe her but me? Why won't they give her a chance? Trust her? Mom, dad, you've got to! Brad and Dell, you especially have got to!

March 2

The old wrinkles are still pissed off at me. They treat me like shit, like I was five years old. Curfew! Points! Withdrawn privileges!

So big question—why so much hate in your mind when love is the only way to straighten things out?

March 3

I'm trying! I'm trying hard to comprehend how it was when my old man was young! Didn't he get the hots like I get? Doesn't he understand what they're doing to me? I'm afraid to even think it but with Debbie being like she is and everything if she can't see me she might start seeing someone else. I couldn't stand that! And I won't let it happen! I don't care what my parents, or anyone else in the whole word, say or do! Judas, what a bleak way to exist. My clothes, my hair, my teeth, my room, *everything* sets them off.

March 4

Today Debbie was feeling extra low. I can only go to school and work and never see her alone. I let her talk me into ripping off a few amphetamines for her. At least with them she can get through the days without always being in tears. I took them out of the bottle Dr. Morrison had prescribed and I was delivering to rich old Mrs. Lawder. I'm sure it's just diet garbage. No biggie.

March 5

Today I had to get Debbie some barbiturates so she can sleep. Man, I hate this! But if I don't get them for her she says she'll get them from Craig. I *won't* lose her to that crotch scratcher. I hate to see her on the merry-go-round but I can get her straightened out once I'm off restriction.

March 7

Freedom! Debbie and I were like two little kids afraid life would run off without us. Her mom was at her aunt's, who is sick, so we cut school and had the whole house to ourselves. Man, did we ever make good use of every room and every bed in it.

March 9

I'm worried about Debbie, she's really using! I'm having a hard time keeping her supplied. I've got to find help for her but I don't know exactly how to go about doing it. 'Ups' all day and 'downs' at night.

April 10

Time goes so fast I can't believe it. Debbie and I are inseparable. We go to church together and to Mutual together and she either has Monday Home Night at my house or I go to hers. We aren't sixteen yet so according to church standards we aren't allowed to officially date, which is kind of funny since we're jumping in and out of the brush every time we have fifteen minutes together. *'Too young to date.'* Ho, ho, ho.

April 12

Today Debbie came to our house for dinner. Everybody was really neat to her. It made me feel guilty as hell, because, all the time they were telling her how nice she looked and how sweet she was and stuff, she was trying to get me to take her down to my bedroom. Sometimes she's like two different people. I love her with a kind of eternal protective love and there's no way I'll throw her out on the street to take care of her habit, but it's getting to where I can't handle my end of it. She handed me a pathetic little note today in school saying she *had to have more* 'ups' and I almost cried when I read it. Practically every other word was misspelled and the punctuation was like someone had stood across the room and thrown periods, commas, etc. She's like a child. She really is! Like a helpless dependent, dumb, dumb, dumb, really dumb in all ways, child. Oh God, what have I gotten myself into? Kendall and Chad, at seven and five, write, read and speak better than she does. But we were *always* treated like adults. I guess we're an unusual family . . . *Unusually* stupid! At least *I am* to have gotten myself in this mess! Can I handle her? Can I handle her habit?

April 14

Oh God, I hate myself. I despise myself. I curse myself, but I had to do it! I've written for information about how and where to get help for Debbie but until I get it . . . Oh God, how could I? Was that really me that went down to the pharmacy an hour early and opened amphetamine capsules and after carefully pouring all the contents into a baggie filled the caps up again with powdered milk? I'm trying to convince myself that

most of the people who use 'ups' don't need them anyway but man it's hard . . . hard . . . hard . . . My dad
wouldn't believe I could ever do anything like that. I
can hardly believe I did it myself.

In a way it's Gregg's fault. He told me about taking
stuff out of his dad's bag. He made it seem so easy;
doctors being so tired and uptight all the time, his old
man had never even noticed or missed anything, especially after Gregg started substituting dried milk or
powdered sugar in the capsules which he emptied.

Man, I can hardly stand the strain of it thinking about
someone with their arm caught in the elevator webbing
and being torn out of its socket in blood and gore and
torn muscles and flesh and the emergency doctor giving
them dried milk or powdered sugar capsules to ease
their pain; and what about the kid I saw one time who'd
been run over right at his crotch by a big old diesel
truck? What if that doctor's kid had . . . Oh crap, this
strain is literally and truly going to drive me bananas.

Why did I do it? Why in hell did I ever, ever, ever
do it? One thing is sure—no matter what, I will never
do it again! Nothing, nobody, could ever make me go
through this hell guilt trip again!

April 23

I'm grounded, but only for two days this time. Lucky
dad thought I was goofing off instead of doing my jan-
itorial chores. Judas, if he had known why I didn't have
my work done at the store, he'd have died. Actually I'm
scared and I don't feel right about substituting and all
that shit but when Debbie begs me to get her some
'uppies' or 'downies,' *I have to. Any way I can. The*

only way I can! I'm hooked on her! I really truly, in the worst way, am hooked on her!

Debbie and Brad and Dell and I are studying about Hare Krishna and Zen and stuff. We've got to find something that will help Deb . . . Brad and Dell are such special buddies. They know I won't leave Deb . . . and I know they won't leave me. It's the only thing that holds me together. Life is really shitty. All the stuff they sent from the Mental Health Center is just so much garbage. Maybe it wouldn't be if Deb would go in herself, but she won't. Sometimes I wish I'd never met her. NO I don't. I couldn't face life without her. She depends upon me so much. She brings out all the good in me . . . and the bad.

> How sad
> That life and growth are based on tears
> And blind are left to lead the blind
> Or fall behind
> To depths of despair
> That have no ending
> Anywhere.

July 15

Tonight I'm really feeling low. At the dinner table dad was telling about Aunt Laurel, who has cancer, and how they just don't seem able to relieve her pain even when they double her dosage of medication. He told about Aunt Laurel crying and begging him to give her something to make her die. That she couldn't, she really couldn't, bear the pain, to please, please give her something to make her die. I got so uptight I spilled my milk in my plate and when the kids laughed I came completely unglued and swore at them. That got everybody off their rockers and now I'm sentenced to my room again. But at least I deserve it this time. I more than deserve it! No doubt dad was dispensing some of the capsules I'd emptied and filled with powdered milk. I wonder how many other people that really need medication are genuinely suffering while we're taking our trips. God, I can't believe that I've been substituting for four months for me and Debbie and Brad and Dell, too—God! How could I? Well, I'm not going to do it anymore, no matter what!!! I'm not! I'm not! We'll have to start going to keggers, or getting someone to make the beer-run for us to the junction or maybe get our stuff off the streets.

Man, I don't know how I got sucked into this whole scene. At first substituting and stealing Darvon and stuff seemed so hard, it about did me in. I cried and had to make myself do it, then it got easy . . . just like they say. Oh God . . . dear, dear, dear God, what can I ever do? I'm going to talk to my seminary teacher. I trust him. He'll help me. He'll help us all. Zen and Hare Krishna and all that crap are just crap. I can't wait for morning to talk to Brother Black.

4:37 A.M.
I just had the nightmare to end all nightmares. I was in the pharmacy department when this wrinkled old decrepit woman hobbled in, gray with pain. She begged dad for some stronger medication to replace the unbearable physical torture I could see she was suffering. He reached for one of the jars where I had traded milk. Gratefully she grabbed the pills and gulped them down. Time passed and she stood there looking at dad with unbelief, the combined agony and torment twisting her

face into even more corkscrew wrinkles. Tears began flooding down her face, tears of total pain and misery. She turned to me and wheezed, 'Son, son, help me . . . help me . . .' *It was only then I recognized her!* It was *mom!* A beaten, tortured shadow of mom, and I had brought the pain and despair to her! She reached over to hug me but I pulled away. The stench of her decaying, already dead, but not dead, body was more than I could bear. I woke myself up with groaning. Oh God, how awful can it get? I hereby swear that I will never make another substitution or steal another pill, or replace a Darvon or anything else. No matter what happens to Debbie, *I am going to go straight!* I'm not into it like she is . . . or am I? I'm dying for a sleeping pill . . . anything to help me escape from this madness. How . . . when . . . did this happen to me? How could I be so unconcerned about the suffering of others? Or is this part of another nightmare—Dear God—I hope so!

July 18

Can you believe the dumb jackass luck? Dad came in early and caught me stealing the pills for Debbie. Judas, he was so mad he was completely out of it. He fired me immediately and said I was a not-to-be-trusted freak and that I wasn't worth the powder to blow me to hell which was right where I was headed, and all shit like that. He said I was a pea-brain disgrace to him and the rest of the family and . . . the thing that hurts the most is that he's right about every damn thing, he's absolutely and completely right. I am just no damn good. No damn good at all. A fifteen-year-old absolute failure and misfit. Willful, rebellious and disgraceful, etc., etc., etc.

How can I ever, in my lifetime, make up for substituting dried milk, aspirin, vitamin C and stuff for really seriously needed medication for all those months?

Lightning flashes 'cross the sky
A bolt that cannot let me by.
It's aimed at me.
The outside storm with bolts and flashes rages
While we are safe and warm within our cages.
A greater storm, by far, screams—indeed it will not rest.
Within my breast.

Almost every night I have this recurring nightmare of mom begging for something to ease her agony. Oh God, it's awful, awful, awful and each night it gets worse.

July 30

I never thought I'd be sent away to a place like this, but crap, I guess they had to do it, especially after dad became suspicious and found out what I'd been doing with the caps. It's the groats! Most of the guys here are weird, druggies, incorrigibles, runaways, or court probation cases. We'd probably all be in juvie hall if our parents didn't have enough money to buy us out. It's a glorified rich man's kid's prison, tennis courts, swimming pool, built-in psychiatrist that nobody ever sees, private tutors even with a regular school set up, but a prison just the same. Every time we look out the windows or go in the yard we're aware of the high fence with the three strands of barbed wire on top. One kid says it's electrified.

I guess what I did was a really big crime because dad and even his pharmacy seem to be in trouble. Mom says they might close him down. Man, seven employees out of work, too, and all my fault.

August 15

Debbie writes nearly every day. I really appreciate that because without her letters I'd go crazy. Her letters are incredibly dumb but maybe her dumbness is what makes her so precious to me, makes me need her so much, maybe she fills my macho insecurity. I could hardly believe that letter was from a fifteen year old.

Oh God! If I could just get over the nightmares about Mom I think I could make it.

August 17

Haven't heard from Debbie in a week but it's O.K. I write to her every day and beg her to write but she doesn't. I guess it's unfair of me to expect her to wait for me while I'm locked away for . . . who knows how long. I guess I'll begin working on improving my intellect, that would make my parents happy. Beginning right now, right this minute, everything I say and think and write must be worthy of my I.Q. Awwww! I'm so fucking bored . . . bored . . . bored . . . So lonely! So alone! Must develop, progress, encourage myself! I'm really going to make a deep study of the Oriental philosophies when I get out of here.

They try to keep us busy, going to full-time school, making pots and macrame, sports, games—my ass is always dragging. It isn't that I do so much but I'm always tired. What can cause that?

Jim Tyler (a nerd) shares the room with Bob London (a fink) and Cal Loomis (a jerk) and me. Jim's parents mortgaged their house to send him here. He's a rip-off artist and he's such a dumb bastard. Man, I don't know how I'm going to cope. I think someone beat all three of them with an ugly stick.

Judas, how I miss Brad and Dell! We've been best, best, best, best, best friends since before first grade. Brad and Dell—I can't think of any of the joys of life without them. Me, and Dell and Brad, on trikes, on bikes, on goats and in cars, the rotten, rebellious, ever looking for trouble trio. I think I'll write a profoundly profound ode to us.

THE JOYS OF THE 'TRIO'

When we were in Boy Scouts, the patrol we organized was called 'The Boner Boys Patrol,' referring to an erection, of course. This may sound perverted but we were indeed quite horny. The flag we had was green with a skull on a maltese cross and our motto, 'Death before Dishonor.' This was an endeavor to 'rip off the system.' Perverting a nice organization such as the Boy Scouts of America was quite an accomplishment, even though we weren't trying to do anything but be ourselves; we didn't realize we were revolutionaries, but we were. (Anyone who happens to read this might get entirely the wrong idea—revolutionary— change for a) the sake of change and b) for the humanization of institutions.) Anyway this was the beginning of our anti-institution campaign.

Even though I didn't know that's what it was until now. . . . The long hair and weird clothes seeking outward changes (we didn't realize that the change must come from within), anti-values establishing own peer group.

Now realization that a) violence leads to repression, b) in order to unsystemize the systems you must work from within the system, and c) you must be open to different points of view in order to become a legend, all the same. And we will yet be legends even as we are apart.

I really cannot help but look back in pride, not at our mistakes but our being and the effect we had on each other and everyone we knew. Brothers in all things. An example of human closeness. For all of the ill that came about, it was an experience of great merit.

Judas, even being profoundly profound is getting boring.

I guess I better stop, but you can't stop life; it just goes on and on! Lonely and ugly and deflating unless you're binged or stoned! You can't do anything to please anybody or say anything to please them or even dress so they'll be happy and give you a smile. Man, they're strict here. I thought my parents were strict, but here you can't even fart without permission.

Oh dear God, life is such an ugly heavy trip, was it meant to be this way?

There must be fulfilling joy and light and hope somewhere. Please God, help lead me there.

Slow time, no time, let the circle go round
A lonely time, a loving time, I'm feeling kinda down

August 28

Today I met Pete. There is something really different about him. Different and fascinating. I feel like a cobra with a mongoose. I just don't know which of us is which. I feel Pete is drawn to me as I am to him, but I don't know why. He's a gorgeous, slick, slim, trim jock, and different somehow than the rest of the teachers but—I don't know—I hope he's not some crazy fairy fruit . . . it's scary but it's exciting.

Debbie has stopped writing altogether so I guess I'm going to have to get my head into something else. But what? What in the world what? In a way I'm kind of glad we broke up. She *used me!* The dirty little whore *used me!* Just like everybody tried to tell me she would. I know she's back on the street with Mark Vrooder again, or whoever is around and will supply her. She alone is responsible for this whole rocked-up mess I'm in. I'd never have done the things I did without her begging and pleading and crying and crying and crying . . . Oh Judas, what a freaked-out hots I was for her, *and I call her dumb! I'm* the dumb bastard that took the fall while she goes right on licking her chops. I've got to get her out of my mind. I won't think about her anymore. I won't! I won't! Only about my parents and what I've done to them . . . and Brad and Dell. Oh dear God, what if my messing around got both of them into the scene where they can't get out either? Please, please God, not that! I was never that dependent upon the stuff myself but everybody's so different.

> Now I lay me down to sleep
> I pray the Lord my soul to keep
> If I should die before I wake

I pray the Lord my soul to take.
Would he? Would even God want me now?

What do you do when every time you see, or think
of a certain chick it breaks your mind into little teeny
pieces and they dribble out your ears? Man it hurts, it
really hurts. It's easy to say 'well, that's life' and try to
play it cool but it still hurts.

Get stoned you say? Well person, it just so happens
you're busted and you couldn't take that chance anyway. Besides, it wouldn't solve the problem only deaden
the pain for a while.

SOLUTION—find another chick. Is it possible? Is
there another one-and-only for me? Only one way to
find out.

She'll have to be cool, not too straight, not too 'the
other way' (like Deb in that respect) and of course,
good lookin' etc., etc. But still. . . . (I wish I had Deb.)

September 2

I still can't read Pete. He teaches history and he relates
to us about like the other wardens called teachers and
advisors. But still, I wish Brad and Dell were here. I
need a friend I really need both my eternal friends! I'm
scared . . . deep inside my guts scared. I don't want to
be here. I want to be home!

I can't sleep. I'm afraid to sleep. Afraid someone will
pounce upon me in the darkness, or tortured death-like
mom, deprived of her life-giving medication, and in her
dead moldy, gray-green shroud will come back again.

Once nights brought warmth and peace and rest,
A lullaby within my breast.

A snoring dog beside my feet,
A snuggling purring kitten by my face,
But, who can trust the human race?

It's 2 A.M. What in hell does anyone do at 2 A.M.? Anyway I just had this neat dream about a girl. Not Debbie, another girl. The exact opposite of Debbie. Judas, she was beautiful, dark and damp. I hope I dream about her again. I do hope I dream about her again!

September 6

This afternoon Pete took me on a work detail and I can't figure out whether he's some kind of a screw-loose or . . . I don't know, he's really got some strange ideas. They sound crazy weird but still I'm so curious to know more I just about wet my pants thinking about when we'll have a chance to talk again. There's no way I could ever dig any of the bull he and another guy, Kurt, are trying to lay on me, but at least it makes me think about something besides my troubles. Pete's into Astara and all forms of the occult. It's so far out it shatters my wavelengths. He talks so easily about intuition, meditation, ESP, auras, life after death, the oversoul, how much karma a person must erase before they are liberated, how they can better influence the world in the new age, how they can recognize their soul mate, mysticism, esoteric science, hidden teachings of the ancients, the equations of life, etc. He says 'an Astarian in need never walks alone.' I need that. Man, right now in my lost cluttered life I really need something like that.

Pete showed me how to meditate and relax for sleeping. I hope it works. It's got to work because I hardly

ever can sleep anymore. Judas I'm so lonely and confused. Jim and Bob and Cal are all such yucks, and it's
the three of them against me. Oh Brad and Dell, I need
a friend!

12:47 A.M.
Pete told me he'd be pulling night emergency duty because old Klamus has the flu. He said I should pretend
sick after 10:30 when he'd be at the nurses' station and
come on down.

The minute I opened his door I could feel . . . I don't
know. He looked at me without speaking, for what
seemed like forever, then at a chair, which soon started
rolling slowly towards me while Pete continued to stare
at it, straining so hard it made creases like the Grand
Canyon in his forehead and squinch wrinkles around
his eyes. I pretended I thought it was some kind of trick
and tried to laugh and find the wires or strings or whatever he'd hooked to it, but of course I couldn't. Pete
moved it absolutely with mental powers. He did! I saw
him do it! I keep telling myself that's ridiculous and
dumb and impossible but he did! He actually did!

After sitting there uncomfortably for another long
period Pete looked down at the little wart on my ring
finger that I've had for—man, I don't even remember
how long. He asked if it was a personal friend and
when I shrugged he suggested we get rid of it.

Patiently he showed me how to synchronize our
breathing and concentrate together. Then he put his
pointer finger on his forehead, then on the wart. Fascinated, I put my pointer finger on my forehead, then
on his. He closed his eyes and a strange guttural low
'ahhhhhh' sound started kind of leaking out of his

mouth. I, completely unbelieving, but out-of-my-head curious joined him.

After a minute Pete got up and pulled the curtains in the little room and locked the door, then we went back to our ahhhhing. Up to this point nothing had happened to my wart and I didn't have any faith that anything would but, Judas, as I look down at my finger now where the wart used to be . . . man, I can't believe it. It did disappear! It really did! It's gone!

The whole concept is spooky . . . but maybe it shouldn't be. Maybe, like Pete says, mind over matter is just something man doesn't understand and is therefore afraid of. I don't think I'm actually *afraid* but I'm . . . man, I'm confused! Why is there this little low-keyed something inside me that's so, all the time, ill at ease around Pete, and yeah, I guess a little-kid-type scared? In some ways scared out of my tree!

September 13
Pete has practically ignored me for a week. I guess he and Kurt told me all that crap just to see exactly how *crackers* I was! I guess what I thought happened really *didn't happen!* But what about the wart? It's still gone! Oh man, all the pressure is making me lose my marbles!

September 14
I dreamed again about her! HER! *HER!!!* Not Debbie! Her! She would make me a better person, not tear all my morals down!

September 16

Today Pete took me into the city to have the school station wagon repaired. I can't recall ever having had a more fantastic day! Maybe it was just because I've been in stir for so long, but then again maybe there is something to all the strange alien stuff he believes so completely. Just because it seems unnatural to my little sheltered provincial mind shouldn't mean anything. Man, it really is heavy thinking. This is the first time I've been emotionally stimulated since I don't know when. To expand my intellect . . . to comprehend things incomprehensible . . . to actually experience other planes of existence that have not even been complete fantasies before. Man, could it possible, conceivable, feasible be? Did Atlantis genuinely once exist? Does it still? I've never been so upped in my life before, even on drugs and booze. I wonder when we will be able to get together again.

September 17

Last night I met Pete after lights out. We talked for hours about my aura, which shows fear and grief and pain. I can't see auras on other people like he does, yet, but Pete says I can learn, actually I really think I saw a soft whitish glow around him, denoting spirituality, security, dependability and honor. I've got to change mine. As my self-conditioning changes, my aura will change. I want to learn everything all at once, but I know I can't. It's so frustrating! Pete is going to help me find myself! My true self! My inner auwa.

September 18

Pete gave me a herb to chew before I go to sleep. He says it will relax me and give me wonderful dreams. It will show me my inner auwa, my own aura and the aura I can yet obtain. I know I saw Pete's aura tonight and also I am beginning to see the dark sinister ones around Cal and Jim and some of the others. It's a new plateau of existence that I didn't even know existed before. Man, it's so strange and exciting.

September 19

Last night I really did experience cosmic consciousness . . . something supernatural. Pete was right! My psychic self is a slumbering cosmic power. It is my link with infinity to be drawn upon at will. It was not like being stoned. I saw bright colors and stuff but it was like I controlled them instead of them controlling me, and I understood the harmony that governs the worlds in space and the tiny atom. Pete had said that the consciousness that directs the physical universe also pulsated in the cells of my being. He was right! Right and wonderful! He will teach me the mastery of life. Oh, I can't wait. Orthodoxy has ruled my thinking far too long. I and the universe are one. There is no division of supernatural and natural. I must . . . I will, control my karma, thereby controlling all things around me and within me.

September 20
2:14 A.M.
Pete is teaching Tom and Dave and me about ESP. He said he would awaken me at 1:47 A.M. and he did! Oh, these wonderful powers that mankind wastes!

NOON

I can't believe it. Just when I'm beginning to adjust, actually find a new way of life, Mr. Durham hits me with the fact that I'm being released in the custody of my parents the end of the month. When he called me into his office I almost started bawling. Now here I am in my room sick with cramps and chills. Going on sixteen and a snotnosed cry baby. Hell, I'm so P.O.'ed and torn with emotions. I want to leave but I don't want to leave. Something inside me is afraid of Pete and his exotic mysterious beliefs. I think deep down I've always known my parents' church was true. I know a part of me has always wanted to go on a mission, and sometimes in church when I hear people bearing their testimonies, even though I'm kind of acting irreverent on the outside, something deep in my pre-life mental programming tells me that what they are saying is true. I'm so-so-so mixed up. Maybe what I really need is a shrink.

It's the middle of the night again and I can't sleep. How can a person really know what's real and what's unreal, what's right and what's not right?

I suspect that the herbs Pete has given me a couple of times, once to chew and once to drink, were some kind of natural hallucinogens, but I couldn't have been hallucinating when I saw him levitate coins and when he woke me to the minute with ESP or the aura bit. Oh Judas, I love and miss my mom and dad and Kendall and Chad soooooooooooo much. We're such a nice neat family and they care so much about me. They've written or called or sent me some little thing nearly every day I've been here and they visited as often as the school would let them. They're so smart. I really should follow their guidance. Both mom and dad went all the way through college on straight scholarships. I'm sure dad would have become a doctor if grandpa hadn't had a stroke his second year of college and needed him for the next couple of years till he could get back on his feet and run the business again. And dear . . . dear . . . sweet mom. How many times she's slept in my room when I've been sick. She always said she just wanted to be near in case, but I know she knew I was scared and I needed her. They're always there when I need them. Even dad slept in my room once when my fever was high. Oh God, how could I have hurt them, let them down, tormented them, humiliated them, disgraced them, brought suspicion upon my most honorable, Christlike, ethical father? And my devoted and gentle mom, who could have gone into scientific research instead of becoming a mother. Dad says she had three companies after her when she graduated, but she preferred to get married and raise a family. She's all the things anyone could ask of a wife and mother. Our home is always clean and it smells good, and she always has time for us, and knows how to listen. I really miss her homemade bread.

All three of us kids could read before we went to school, and we could count the vegetables she put in the salads and the ingredients she put in the cookies, and we knew the color of eyes and pies and french fries and *wise* men. Even the rhyming thing she taught us when we were little more than infants. It was a fun game then to improve our vocabulary, but now . . . Now I don't know what I'd do without my poems and my song lyrics. Oh thank you, mom! I'm really going to show both you and dad how grateful I am when I get out of here.

> You gave me life
> Then put my hand in yours and led me on my way
> Till I rebelled and lost myself.
> Please do not let me go.
> I need you so.

I will be glad to get home . . . GLAD! GLAD! GLAD! Happy, secure, repentant glad. I never did belong in this hole. Brad and Dell and I have all done crummy mean little rotten things all through our lives but we aren't second-class reject retards. I love my family, my home, God, my country, Dad, Chad and Kendall, Mom and apple pie, and homemade bread . . . yumm . . . homemade bread!

I'll be glad to get home. Most of the kids here are misfits from broken homes or they're just so rebellious nothing can touch them. With me I just kind of got sidetracked. I've got to get my priorities in order once again and I'll be O.K. Without Debbie hassling my head I can make it, but what about when I see her? I don't know how it's possible to love and hate somebody so much at the same time. I honestly don't know whether I'll want to kill her or hug her if I ever see her again. I've asked Dell and Brad about her in a number of letters but they always answer all my other questions and avoid that one. Mom wouldn't lie to me and she says she hasn't heard anything, but she doesn't have her ear to the street.

September 30

I hate it here! I hate the food, and the discipline, and the 'please sir may I go to the bathroom, sir, please'—the whole rinky-dink mini-prison set up. I even hate Pete and his Ouija-board fortune telling that made me think he was something special. He's just another big puke, but at least he made life bearable while I served my term. I won't need him on the outs. I'm going to run so straight I'll never have to see that hurt look in my mom's eyes again, or that frightened, tense, hold-back stance that my dad always takes when I've about driven him to the end.

Judas, I hate to admit it even to myself but sometimes I've done things just to hurt my parents, because I was hurting I wanted to hurt them too . . . I must make a commitment that I will never do that again. I want to belong! I've got to work to belong!

October 9

Been home nine days now and sometimes I don't fit in any better here than I did in the Pine Boys' School.

October 10

I'm hurting so bad I don't know if I should scream or beat myself or throw up. God, tell me, how can people who are supposed to love me and care for me and protect me do this to me? Aunt Meg and Uncle Carter and Aunt Ruth and Uncle Jim came over to dinner and we were just sitting there talking about how uptight the world was getting. I tried to explain a little to them about Transcendental Meditation and Cosmic Realization for inner peace and I can't believe how they all cut me and made fun of me. It was almost savagely ritualistic. Superficious old dumb squares, they didn't know anything about it and they didn't want to learn, all they wanted to do was condemn, hurt, cut, maim. I wasn't trying to say TM or CR would take care of all the world's ills or that they should give up their own beliefs . . . only to implement them. Oh God, how could they be so mean to me? How could they so cruelly, knowingly hurt me? Each taking turns torturing me while the others all sat around and laughed, vicariously enjoying my suffering. I know now how Christ must have felt when they were preparing him and nailing him on the cross.

If that is what Christianity is all about, I must find something better. I must find out who I really am! Not who *they* say I am!

I am a child of the universe. I am a person, self-made, custom-made, handmade. Not seeing all and therefore not judging all.

I am what I am for myself, to please myself and bring good vibrations to others. Fine, absolute, inquiring, acute, working. Unstable at times but still expanding, creating, producing, having, sharing, being, loving, knowing, losing, gaining, happening. Established now, not so alone, but lonesome. Original, a feeling, an organism, an orgasm, a closeness, a level, a conflict.

A disciple, a follower, a leader, a speaker, a person of untold but defined absoluteness and relativeness. Eyes alive, mind still growing, long hair flowing . . . (inside) hurting heart beating.

October 12

When I got home from school there was a phone message that I should call Pete. It really zinged me. We talked for about an hour. Dad will go straight up the wall when he gets the bill, but he can just hang it in his ear because . . . Oh Judas, Pete's got me even more confused than ever. Something inside me could buy the Astro stuff and the Cosmic Concept . . . but witchcraft, that seems too childish and scary storylike . . . But he did . . . he really did . . . right over the phone levitate the pen. He says white witchcraft is of God? To me it's like Satan appearing as an angel of light or some weird thing. I wish I could talk to Pete in person.

October 16

I cut out and hitchhiked up to see Pete for a couple of days. I had to! It was like a magnetic force. Exciting as hell. Now that I'm home and *grounded again* nothing seems real or exciting. It's like some dumb midnight movie, or I was half stoned or something. Pete wants me to get Brad and Dell in. He said he could feel good vibes from their pictures. Oh hell, when I'm with him everything makes so much sense . . . when I'm away it's so much shit.

October 17

Brad and Dell and me cut our last two classes and went down to the lake. Mom's at a convention so I 'borrowed' her car. At first they both laughed when I started to tell them about Cosmic Consciousness but I understood because I remembered how uncomfortable I'd been when I was first introduced to it. Pete told me to be sure and not bring in the witchcraft part until after they'd been in a couple of weeks at least. He said that the innerata has to grow like the outside body, that you don't start out with heavy things that can't be digested mentally. First it has to be milder more palatable stuff, sort of like a baby starting with pablum and milk—they couldn't take steak at first.

Judas, I know if Pete had thrown witchcraft at me the first time, I'd have told him in no uncertain terms to blow it out his rear end. It's funny how hypnotic the concepts are though once you get into them. Brad and Dell both seem as curious and fascinated as I was. I'm glad! It's not fun to be into things alone.

In some little way I'm worried about what I'm getting Brad and Dell into though, because at first it's inno-cent, unhurtable inquisitiveness then . . . I don't know, it's dumb but it's compelling, like you've *simply got to know* what's the next step. Like you're, in some way that you can't understand, being drawn in a direction you're not really willing to go. Oh crap, now I'm phi-losophizing like the old man. HE can take an hour and a half to say 'How do you like the rain?' explaining how cirrus and stratus and cumulus clouds work . . . how each is a mass of condensed water vapor like tiny drops of water or ice crystals . . . and on and on into forever crapland. He's always been like that. I don't want to be like that too.

October 18

Today a letter and a bunch of junk came from Pete. It's weird but my first impulsive inclination was to burn it . . . isn't that childish? Shit, it was almost like I was afraid.

October 19

There is something hypnotic and right about Pete's people and his teachings. I'm thinking more and more about them. It's like they and I can communicate in ways besides letters and phone calls. I wish I knew more . . . In some ways I'm repelled in even the little I know . . . it's dumb . . . I'm scared and repelled, yet indeed at the same time, drawn and, almost out of my head, curious. I think I'll forget it, all of my background and teaching tells me Pete and his concepts are wrong . . . But what is wrong? Pete says 'wrong' is only programming . . . conditioning . . . tradition . . . Man, I wish I had a sleeping pill.

October 20

I'm sitting here in my room so confused I don't know what the hell way is up. Pete's letter today has about blown me away and Brad and Dell are both working at the market so I've no one to talk to.

I've got to get a job! I have too much vacant time on my hands, that's what is giving me these apprehensions and . . . Oh crap, I'm just bored and confused and neither kid nor man, neither fish nor fowl, neither beast nor vegetable, neither mineral nor vitamin . . . see, I'm really cracking. No, I'm beyond cracking, I'm shattered. I'm lost. I'm fragmented. Everyone belongs, knows where they're going but me. I am the only lonely . . . how lonely . . . how sad . . . how unfulfilling . . .

I wish I hadn't left my guitar at Brad's.

Can people have daymares as well as nightmares? That's what Pete's letter conjures up, daymares. Oh crap, crap, shit, crap, shit!

October 29

Dad got me a job at the stationery store. But I still can't get my head out. Man, life can be a downer! Pete has sent two missionaries to Brad and Dell and me. Man, that seems strange, *missionaries* connected with witchcraft! . . . I can see auras now and I can levitate very very small things and my auwa is taking more form but . . . I WANT OUT!

November 1

Halloween was ghoulish. How can you be stoned without being stoned? It wasn't real. IT WAS NOT REAL! I'm hallucinating. I'm afraid. I won't even drink anymore.

November 2

Could I be having flashbacks? I haven't used for two or three months now. I've written a ten-page letter to Pete. Oh Judas, he's got to be able to explain it. I can't go on this way.

November 4

Brad, Dell and I drove up to see Pete. He says we're being pushed by the intruders because we aren't doing enough for the order. He gave us a list of the kids he knows about who are investigating, or in, in our area. I was absolutely and beyond belief amazed at how many there are. Twenty-five in our own school that we never dreamed about, and each one of us is obligated to bring two more in this year if we are to have the strength of the group to combat *outside influences*. Oh crap, I don't want to bring anyone else into this shit hole, but I can't stand the outside pressures either.

I thought I was unhappy before. I was just a stupid young kid that didn't know what happiness was. I was like a snot in a candy store who not only wanted all he could eat, but the whole thing. Life is stupid! Stupid! Stupid! Or at least to this point, mine is.

Pete says that happiness beyond belief lies only two steps, or days, beyond now. That we are just being 'tried and tested' to see if we are worthy of O. I guess I'll try that much more. Just that much! IF it doesn't work I'll go back to the old ways . . . my father's ways, though I do not belong either place. Brad and Dell are going through a shit time too. Two more days! I will only wait *two more days!*

2 A.M.

I just finished the book Pete sold me, and went through the nightly rituals he suggested. Made me feel upped, but somehow mentally disjointed.

One after another I have intrusions of unwanted family into my room. My auwa nightly rituals are the only thing that make me feel better, and the strange sounds of the ancient expressions as they gurgle out of my throat.

November 5

So today was another Sunday. Had a far-out discussion on evolution in Sunday school today. 'Bro.' Black got all bent out of shape, etc. And I got really bombed. At any rate today was just another Sunday.

* * *

all alone today again, radio, books, and loneliness, are the daily fare.

develop, progress, encourage all myself, but unhelpful intrusions of unwanted people make head gathering hard, put on defense, don't let it down or they might try to get in.

'On a Sunday morning sidewalk I'm wishing God that I was stoned, cause there's something in a Sunday that make a body feel alone.'

November 6

Pete was right! Two days later and all is right with the world. Is it just more of what Kendall calls 'coincidence-a-dinkies?' Anyway everything is going so well I can hardly stand it. We had a basketball game this afternoon and beat Longshore by one point. One free basket! The first time we've beat them in ten years. Imagine, by one point! Man, everybody was so excited it was like a rock concert. Hugging, screaming, kissing, whistling, laughing, going crazy, even teachers and the principal. He was jumping up and down like a little kid who had to go to the bathroom. We were all on a natural happy high. It was better than dope or booze or anything.

Me and Dell and Brad were sitting about halfway back in the gym and Dell straightened his body and we hoisted him above our heads and passed him all the way down to the playing floor and then back to the top benches and down again. He had his arms up with a pompom in each hand and one between his feet. It was wild! Crazy-happy-fun wild.

At 7:30 tonight we had our interstate debate team run-off . . . naturally modest, humble me won! Man, I sweat to win that one though because it was about capital punishment which I'm for and I had to take the opposite side. That always gives me the super-sulphur sweats, but I know it's good for me too! IT takes control and discipline that are deadly hard—when you have to plead a cause you don't in the least believe in.

After the debate we had a dance. I went stag because it was late but took Marie home, with Bill and Jo Ellen. Naturally the long-cut stopping off at Make-Out Flats for a while. Marie is O.K. for a night but I wouldn't want to date her, she's . . . I don't know, she's so aggressive and loud and hyperactive, sort of like she's afraid tomorrow isn't going to come or something. I like girls who are a little more together, not so frayed and rowdy. Maybe it's just the way I was brought up. Mom's idea is that everyone is trying to get attention, but that intelligent persons get theirs by doing something worthwhile, beneficial to himself and the community.

November 7

More goodness! Janie met me for lunch in the cafeteria. I was chosen by Mr. Borough to represent our class in the forum Speak Out. I heard that Debbie had moved to California to live with an aunt whose husband is with the juvie department. That should get her unkinked and out of my head.

I'm going to quit letting things I can't understand hassle me. Man, the sun is shining like it's just been let out of a dark cave, or is it *me* shining inside myself because I've come out. Anyway, wow! Wowwie! Wow!

Golly gee I'm glad I'm me
There's no one else I'd rather be.
I smile on every bird and tree.
Life is a ball. I'm in love with me!
And the music is great too!

November 10

Dad took me to Denver. Man it was cool. We were like
buddies. Not me, the kid, getting orders from him, the
man. Dad was giving a paper about some research he
was doing at the University in his spare time. I was so
proud of him! I guess it was the first time since I was
a little kid that I remembered what 'family' really is.
It was like I was a little part of *him*. Proud for him,
scared for him, praying for him. Supportive of him.
And he said my presence gave him strength and courage and security. It was so neat I want to cry. We really
were one and I want to be just like him! Strong, intelligent, trustworthy, honorable, supportive, credible.

For the last few years I've just been looking at *his*
faults, everybody's faults but my own! No more, man—
no more.

November 23

I feel as stuffed as the turkey! Janie and I, and Dell and
Pat, and Brad and Laura (who's old enough to drive)
went tubing after dinner, then I must admit I waddled
down to the refrigerator and polished off another couple
of meals at one sitting. It's been a nice relative get-
together Thanksgiving. I really am thankful for all my
blessings. Mom put five tables choo-choo fashion on
the end of the dining room table; they extended halfway

into the living room. Man, it was like a beehive. All twenty-seven of us talking at once. Discussing apathy and violence, church and pornography, busing and lack of integrity, and everything else. Words were flying and opinions were exploding and theories were being expounded. Sometimes Uncle Robert or someone raised their voices till the windows rattled and the china in the dining room cabinets shook. It was positively wonderful! I guess because for the first time I *felt* like one of the adults instead of one of the dumb kids! and I DIDN'T GET MY FEELINGS HURT ONCE! although at one point or another everyone disagreed loudly. We were all interrupting and bringing forth different ideas that were accepted, rejected or torn up and discarded. It was almost like a community debate. Disagreeing or having differing opinions was part of the fun! Everybody just throwing concepts like snowballs, some hitting, some missing but none maiming. I guess I really used to maim my own self! I certainly know that nobody in this fantastic, super intelligent family would ever *try to hurt me!* In the past I was just supersensitive, downright paranoid! My family and extended family are the most supportive people in the world! Just as they ought to be! Just as I desire to be! Just as I will be! Man, it's only November 23 and I'm making resolutions already!

Happy long evening! I'm like a big fat purring cat stretched out here on my bed. I just talked to Janie and we're going to meet in the morning at McDonald's for a McMuffin. Ugh, even the thought of food is yuck . . . but by morning, knowing me, I'll be hungry again. Janie is supportive like my family, also smart, actually in a couple of my starred classes at school. It's nice to date someone I can talk to about something other than sex and drugs. She really is a nice girl. I hope our relationship grows into something.

November 24

I don't know what's happened to me. I woke up this morning grateful 'cause I'm able to put my socks on. Grateful I can see, hear, smell, think, appreciate. Grateful I haven't got a cold, with my nose clogged up, grateful I don't have a blister on my toe or a sliver in my finger.

At breakfast mom hugged me, scratched through my head like she used to when I was little and made me my very favorite blueberry pancakes.

It's been a neat day. I read all of Chad's 977 favorite books to him and played Battleship with Kendall and Monopoly with mom and dad after dad got home.

The Thanksgiving leftovers were almost better than yesterday's feast. Man, I'm glad I wasn't an original pilgrim on their first Thanksgiving when they only had seven kernels of corn each.

Janie came over for a while, then she had to go to her married sister's.

Brad and Dell stopped by and we listened to records and tapes and rapped about when we were little. Man, we were a funny trio. Still are! Just being together makes us feel funny and free and good.

Last year when our Explorer leader took us up the canyon for a few days I'm sure we three had a better time than the rest of the whole group put together. It was so funny when Old Brad was trying to build a raft in his altogether and got his bum sunburned, so sunburned he couldn't sit down or sleep on his back for days; and when we put axle grease in the pan with the gravy; and caught the squirrel in a trap and zipped it in Brother Brown's sleeping bag. I've never seen a big guy move so fast and so far in so short a time. We were always doing things like that. Man, what stories I'll have to tell my kids. As good as the ones mom and dad tell us about when they were growing up—Mom on a ranch in Wyoming and Dad, with all his relatives, in a town so little it isn't even on the map anymore. Once we drove out to see where gramps had had his combination grocery store, pharmacy and gas station. It's now part of a copper mining dump.

I guess all people have fun when they're kids if they just let themselves . . . and the good and the bad are both always there and we're gonna see what we look for. Mom and dad are right, I really have been a negative miserable pain-in-the-butt bastard . . . although they wouldn't put it exactly that way. But I'm grown up now! Almost sixteen, almost old enough to legally have wheels. I think I'll start saving my money so I can buy some kind of a junker and fix it up so on *that* day . . . wow . . . Man, I'll be out of the garage with that shiny mover at the first crack of dawn like a bat out of hell. Me and my wheels.

Around and around and around they go
Ever so fast, ever so slow.
Taking me from my childish past.
To a mature fulfilled future that ever will last . . . and last . . . and last. . . .

Gas, insurance, license—it's gonna take a lot of bread to support a car.

I read once how much the guy who wrote the Dr.

Seuss books makes. Judas, I think maybe I'm going to
write a Dr. Seuss type book for teen-age nonreaders:

> Dick spit
> And hit
> The teacher in the eye
> Dick split
> And so did I
> Didn't want to see
> The teacher cry.

That's gross, but seriously I wonder if nonreading
teen-agers don't deserve to have some simple 'their
type' books written. Books with neat pictures and a
kind of underground flavor:

> Jane smelled bacon burning
> And quick shut off her gas.
> Dick smelled bacon burning
> And quickly moved his ass.

Publishers and stuff wouldn't even know 'bacon
burning' was 'pigs' or 'cops' coming. So that's not it!
Sometimes things sound so simple you just *know* you
could do better, till you try, then it's a wipe out. But if
at first you don't succeed keep on trying—you'll suck
a seed. Oh yuck, sheeeeeeet.

> See Jane run.
> See Dick run.
> Jane does not try to run fast.
> See Dick catch Jane.
> See what Dick does to Jane.

No, you are too little to see.
That is only for Dick and Jane and me . . .

Oh crap . . . I've got such a dirty mind. I should be able to control it better than I do, but Man, *it's really hard!* Oops—there I go again! Once I remember a speaker at a conference said that bad thoughts are like birds . . . we can't keep them from flying over our heads but we can keep them from nesting in our hair. That's my problem! I not only let them make nests in my hair *I encourage them!* I wonder if shaving my head would help? Let's see . . . that same speaker said I should start substituting, singing a good song for a degrading thought . . . What song? What song has elevating words?

Raindrops keep falling on my head.
Or have I really wet the bed.

Oh crap, give up. Think about cars. Think about *the* car!

November 25

I can't believe girls! Janie came unglued because I didn't want to ball. It isn't really that I don't want to. I want to like hell but I can't let myself get into another relationship right now. She thinks it's because I don't love her, but I do! I like her and love her both! Judas, women!

Brad and Dell both say that they have to fight girls off too.

Dad's always throwing in these little sex things when we talk and telling me how I have to protect girls and how the guys are the aggressors and all that. He doesn't know how much things have changed. I would have liked living in his day. It's like you're not being manly or you can't or you're a queer if you just plain don't want to, or you're waiting—or . . . I don't know what it is, but right now I'm just going to cool my jets no matter what! I'm going to pay more attention to my church standards. I'm going to be more what my parents want me to be and what the real me wants to be!

November 26

I'm getting mellow in my old age. Here I am tending kids and I don't even mind, actually it has in a way been fun. Kendall popped corn and we played 'I Doubt It' and watched TV and it was just like it ought to be in a family . . .

Chad burned his hand on the pan Kendall was melting butter in and he didn't scream or have a fit or anything, he just told me I was the neatest and smartest brother in the world when I put his fingers in a bowl filled with ice cubes and water.

I like those two little guys! I love them! I like being with them and being supportive and protective. I'm sounding like a man instead of a boy . . . at last! At last!

November 28

I was chosen to represent the school in the state Speak Out contest. Imagine, one kid out of a school and *I'm it!* Man, I'm so proud I can hardly button my shirt over my swelled chest or get my hair to stay down on my swelled head. I keep saying, 'Oh it's nothing,' but inside I want to scream, 'I'm important! I'm important! Hey look at me, everybody!'

Dad, mom and the rest of the family are so proud of me. It's special to do something that gives them pleasure and pride for a change.

December 1

I won. Man, what an ego trip. Maybe I'll go into law, at least now I definitely know I want to stay on the debating team.

December 5

Brother Niels, my seminary teacher, asked me if I'd be the narrator at the Christmas program. That kind of hurt because these past few months I've skipped his class oftener than I've attended it and when I did go I wasn't really listening, my mind was drifting off in any direction but the one he wanted. But anyway, it is a compliment and another ego high.

December 9

Tiffany asked me to the Preference Ball. It's the neatest thing that's ever happened to me. She could go out with any guy in this school. She and Tamara Thomas are the two foxiest chicks here. I'm thinking about them both fighting over me. Sometimes fantasies are better than real life.

December 14

Tiffany was the most fantastic fox at the dance. Man, I was so proud of her . . . and of me! Wow, my confidence doth wax strong . . .

I must be doing something right. Tamara asked Brad and Dell went with Georgia Mills, she's not much to look at but she really is fun, and Girls' League President. The whole thing was wow! Tammy's a year older than the rest of us so she took her mom's car. It's kind of funny to be chauffeured about by a girl but at this age I guess we all pretty much have to take what we can get. You can't rip off a car for a Preference Ball.

December 17

Imagine an A+ on a seminary test. Me, the one that thought I couldn't stand anything about the class. Actually Brother Niels is pretty fascinating now that I've started listening to him. If I shut my eyes the material makes a most fantastic part of the TEN COMMANDMENTS movie. I saw it when I was a little bitty snipper and I've never forgotten. Man, those were exciting days. I wouldn't have liked living in them, except of course, if I'd been a pharaoh or something, but come to think about it, the pharaoh didn't make out too well in the end either.

December 18

GROUNDED AGAIN! But at least this time it's only for a week and I gave the punishment to myself. I guess 'borrowing' mom's car and then getting the fender bent wasn't the smartest thing in the world to do. I shouldn't have been showing off but a kid driving a big old long black Cadillac has to either show off or act dead. Judas, $50 for the repair, at least I just have to pay the $50 deductible . . . Fifty dollars . . . oh the pain! Well, anyway, it was pretty straight of dad to ask me what I thought he should do as punishment.

December 19

Being grounded is giving me time to learn the Christmas script but it's so, so, so boring! I've got this damned cold and my nose is running like a faucet and my head is clogged up and my chest rattles and groans when I cough like I'm nine hundred years old. The stereo won't work and there's nothing on TV except soaps and game shows which I hate. Dad is working, the kids are at school and mom is up staying with her sister in Wyoming for a few days. Aunt Kay is only thirty-one years old and has terminal cancer. It's really rough with her four little kids. . . . kind of scary too because our family seems to have a predisposition towards cancer on both sides. I never say anything, but every time I get a lump or a mole or a wart I wonder . . . prostate cancer is . . . oh crap, there's no need to think about morbid things like that. Indeed, to be more realistic I should, now that I've got the time, evaluate my priorities in life and get myself somewhat straightened around.

Set goals . . . disciplines . . . I *know* where I came from, what I'm doing here, where I'm going! I just haven't been doing much to attain. Oh I made it at the Speak Out and now I'm working on the pageant, but the every minute of every day stuff I'm falling down on.

To evaluate:

I respect and honor my father. He does the very best he can with his abilities, physically, mentally, emotionally and spiritually . . . and he's extremely together about most things! Man, I just fragment when things don't go my way or I can't control them. He was so cool when we were skiing and Dell took the uncontrolled fall and hit the tree. Dad had his leg set with his broken ski and a temporary sled stretcher made out of branches and his remaining ski and ski poles, and us all calmed down in the midst of that sudden blizzard, like nothing had ever happened. Man, *that* is cool. And the time when we were going to California and saw the car wreck. . . . It was like he was Jesus the way he calmed down the hysteria and screaming and stuff, and stopped the bleeding and quieted the two little kids that were hurt. I was practically no help at all. I just wanted to go out in the cactus and throw up or just stand around and gawk like everybody else that stopped. Yes, there is much in him to admire, that I should pattern my life after.

Mom also; gentle, kind, a little overweight but pretty in an old way, intelligent. I'll be lucky if I find a wife like her when I grow up. She makes such good bread!

Kendall: not too bright, mom works hard with him but even learning his times tables was Herculean. I love that word. Someone used it at the Speak Out . . . Herculean . . . isn't that descriptive? I've got to work harder at retaining really descriptive words, for

Maybe I'll be a doctor.

Maybe I'll be a lawyer.

Maybe I'll be a scientist.

Maybe I'll be an oceanographer or a biologist or a pharmacist.

Maybe I'll be a writer. I wonder how I'd go about

that or what I'd write about. *Not* a TV Jamie at fifteen who gets a teacher pregnant and . . . I wonder why decisions in life are so difficult.

Brad has *always* wanted to do something mechanical, be an engineer, own a garage, race cars, fly planes . . . whatever . . . but at least he knows in which direction he's going. Dell, well, he's more like me. I'm not sure his parents can afford to send him to college, though. His old man is just a carpenter, Dell wants more . . . but . . . who the hell knows what the future is going to bring. That isn't right! I must be more precise in my writing as well as my thinking if I'm going into any of the above fields. *One molds and makes their future!* At least if they want one of any consequence.

Chaddy. I love that little flipper. He can be so neat when he's good and lovable . . . and such a rotten little I-can't-stand-him stinker when he's not.

Conclusion: With my mental, physical, and spiritual attributes, coming from this provincial, protective-type town, with my supportive, honorable parents and peers, and my caring, conscientious teachers, there is not one reason why I should not be happy and successful in any field of endeavor I see fit to choose.

Happiness and success, here I come! Watch out for me! I'm like a comet piercing through the black darkness of ignorance. I'm going to work harder on my spiritual growth too. I'm sure that's what me and Brad and Dell need. We've all been sort of drifting spiritually since that last big surge just before we were twelve.

Man, I feel good! Just kind of getting myself in sync with what I've got, where I am and where I'm going is a neat feeling. I can do it! I can! I can! I can! Now, I just have to find out *WHAT* it is I'm going to do.

I've just reread today's entry. What a dissertation!

Man, sometimes I even impress myself. I guess I can admit it here, I'm pretty neat. Good bod, good mind, good me! Wow! What have I been taking? Does orange juice ferment?

December 22

The pageant was fantastic. I can't believe that everything went off so well, with so few hitches. No loudspeaker problems, no light problems, no cast problems . . . well, at least at the final production. The place was filled to overflowing and with the speakers put up all around the audience, when they used them in the last 'Hallelujah Chorus,' man, it was like we were all being smothered in music; not really smothered, more baptized, immersed. Carl, from the music shop, had brought the amplifiers he used with his rock group. I still get goose bumps and sweaty palms when I think about it. Sweet little Chad looked up at me with his innocent childish eyes shining after it was over, and asked me seriously if 'really-for-true' angels were singing with us. That about wiped me out. Wow, a tear just dropped down on my journal even now.

December 27

I've had a relapse of my cold plus the flu and I slept almost the full time of Christmas. Throwing up, diarrhea, then sleeping . . . the story of my life for the past few days. This afternoon is the first time I've even felt like climbing up through the crawl hole in the attic to bring you down, which should make you feel good if journals have any feelings. I'm getting sick again . . . oh shit!

January 5

Dell's dad just got the contract to frame in five big apartment and condominium units in Las Vegas. He'll be there six months so he's taking the family down. They'll live with Dell's great-aunt who has an old big house there. Dell says it's in kind of a crummy area but . . . Judas, I'm going to miss him. He's like my brother, in some ways more than a brother. He's my friend! My very very best friend, well, at least he and Brad are. The Three Nephites. We've been living kind of like them for the last couple of months; being considerate, trying to help others anonymously when possible. It's made us feel so good and we've been so close, almost closer than ever. Oh crap, it's going to be the groats without Dell. It's like Chaddy or Kendall were leaving, confidentially, maybe even more painful . . .

I'm thinking about skiing tonight with dad. There is so much snow on the mountains. Here in the valley it's almost like spring. Skies blue and clear but clouds resting over Whitecap. Maybe it's snowing up there right now though it's only twenty minutes away.

But I don't feel like skiing. The shock of Dell's leaving is like a physical punching out. I guess this is the first time in my life I've ever felt a trauma and really known what it was. Man, it's bad! Kind of like it infiltrates your body in every pore. I can't eat, I can't concentrate. It's almost even worse than when I broke up with Debbie . . . different . . . but just as black and lonely and lost and a it's-not-true, I-won't-believe-it kind of feeling.

I guess I'll work late tonight. Mr. Stokes is doing inventory and I might as well be miserable working as be miserable spending my hard earned money; besides the news even made me uncoordinated. In basketball practice I missed every single shot I tried to make . . . that's not me! I'm not good but I'm not that rotten! Oh shit, I guess this, like everything else bad in life, will pass, besides Las Vegas isn't that far away. Mom said I could go down some weekend and stay and Dell's folks said he could bus it up here occasionally. In a way I feel like a fruit I hurt so bad. I want to hug Dell and cry on his shoulder and tell him how rotten it's going to be, just me and Brad . . . two whats? Judas, I'm acting like Dell's dead, or dying, what a bean-brain, what a selfish yuck.

It's going to be a lot worse for him than for me. I should think about him. He won't have anything . . . anyone . . . Me and Brad will both be here and all the kids we've always grown up with. For him it will be like me at the Pine Boys' School. Oh please, God, not that! Don't let him get so lonely and confused that he'll . . .

I gotta go to work . . .

12:30 A.M.
Man, inventory is hard—worked from 4:30 till past midnight and on a school night. Mom's going to be hopping!

January 6
Dell's last night here so mom let him and Brad sleep over. It was like the olden days, only better! We had pillow fights and ate everything that was loose in the house even though mom had gone to the market and bought what she said was enough junk food for the American army and navy both. And dad threatened

Kendall and Chad to stay the heck away from my room, because he knew we wanted to be alone.

Brad wanted to be funny so he brought his electric blanket over and put it inside his sleeping bag. Right after he'd gone to sleep I woke up Dell and we turned it on high then snuggled down to see what would happen. In a few minutes Brad fought his way out of the bag, sweating and swearing. We pretended we were asleep while he turned off his bag, opened the window a crack and made himself a pallet on the floor. Fighting hard to control our snickers, Dell and I waited until he'd gone to sleep again, then opened the window wide, closed the heat vent in the room and waited for episode two. Sure enough pretty soon we heard old Brad scratching around looking for more covers and the switch to his electric blanket. Practically strangling to keep from laughing, we again waited until he went to sleep, then turned up the heat in the room, turned up his blanket high and waited for the explosion. Brad must have really been groggy with sleep because again he just turned down the blanket and squirmed out on top of the covers. Beside ourselves, Dell and I turned off the blanket, opened the window and waited. Within minutes Brad came up slugging. It had taken him a long time to figure out what was happening but when he did he was ready to hit both of us up the side of the head. It was half an hour before we could get him to see how funny it was, then we all rolled on the floor and got hysterical. It's a good thing my room is upstairs and mom had had Kendall and Chad sleep in the guest room in the basement. We'd have awakened the dead if we lived close to a cemetery.

Man, that was funny, so funny that neither Dell nor

I dared go back to sleep. We knew Brad would find some way to get even with us, and did he ever!

He knows I go stinky when I first get up in the mornings so he put apple butter all over the toilet seat and then pulled the bathroom curtains and unscrewed the light. I got up all groggy eyed and made my early trek to the john, sat down, and about blew my mind. Brad, who'd been waiting, jumped up like an ape on the sink and screwed in the bulb, bringing to view the brown turd-looking goop all over my bottom and running down my legs. I wanted to kill him. It wasn't funny! Not then anyway.

All through breakfast Dell waited to see what was going to be his come-uppance . . . nothing came . . . lunch passed . . . no problems . . . then Dell's last class, gym. He went to put on his tennis shoes and squishhhhhhhhhhhh. Brad had somehow stuffed the right toe with dog-do. The whole class about went crazy as Dell hopped off to the showers with dog shit oozing out from between his toes. Mad! He was mad—dog mad! He and I had known all along we couldn't get away with anything, but, man, dog shit; only one of us would think of something like that!

Was there ever such a terrible but terrific trio? I wonder, will my kids and their kids feel this same fantastic forever-whatever-affinity?

January 11

Dad is out of his head worried about mom. For the first few days they thought her fever was from a cold or the flu or something but now it's up to 103 or 4 and she stayed in the hospital overnight. They can't find anything. If something doesn't change by tomorrow they are going to do an exploratory. Judas, I can't stand that, them just cutting mom open and plowing around her insides trying to find out what isn't working right or what's infected.

I know mom'd give her life for me. I'm just lying here wondering if I'd give mine for her. Oh Judas, I'm so afraid I wouldn't, I'm almost sure I wouldn't. I'm such a selfish, egotistical, self-centered yuck. God's plan of making parents was such a wonderful one. They love kids in a deeper way than kids love them. I wonder if when I'm a parent I'll love so completely and without reservation. After I'd been rolling with Debbie and . . . Judas, I hate to even think about it, even though it's always sneaking about somewhere in the back alleys of my mind . . . substituting in dad's pharmacy, even *then* they both loved me without reservation. Oh they hated what I'd done but they've always, always *loved me!*

Crap, I'm crying like a little two-year-old girl . . . but I feel so bad . . . so bad. . . . Dad honors his family name. It's part of his religion, part of his background, part of his heritage . . . and me, that honored special family name didn't mean shit to me when I was only interested in my own needs. I didn't think about his, and my, ancestors crossing the plains, doing without, being maligned and mistreated and martyred. . . . No, only about me . . . the big fancy jock trying to make his woman happy by any means.

Not that it was easy that first time. I remember my tee shirt got absolutely wet with perspiration I was so nervous, and my head was pounding like someone was trying to drill a well inside . . . and my stomach . . . I remember the knots and wrenches and the fear that I was going to throw up all over the whole counter. Another strange thing, I'd never been bothered much about stinking when I sweated but man, I could hardly stand myself then. It was like I was sweating rotten egg gas. That's weird, isn't it? That even my chemical balance was upset? . . . or that evil? . . . or . . . oh Judas, I'm crumbling my crackers.

What if mom dies? Who will make the bread? I don't think I could exist without her homemade bread. It smells so good, and . . . see, even now I'm thinking of me. Not her, not dad, not poor little Kendall and Chad. What would they do? I'm big enough to make it on my own but . . . I wonder if dad would have Aunt Joyce, who just lost her husband, come and live with us. . . . Oh I hope not, she's such a fanatic about having everything clean and straight. She can't stand a gum wrapper in a waste basket or a milk glass on the sink. What if dad remarries? Who? Would she be good to Kendall and Chad? I know whoever she was, she couldn't love them as much as mom.

Oh God, here I am thinking about things like mom's already being dead. That's faith for you. But between Dell leaving and mom so . . . whatever . . . I can't stand it. I feel like my head and chest and stomach and everything else is going to explode! Oh God, help me stand it.

3 A.M.

I don't know when I've ever prayed so long so hard. God just can't let mom die now. We need her too much. Kendall and Chad and dad need her. I'm not worth her love. But I'm going to be! If mom gets well I'm going to make her proud and happy. I'll have a grade point average that is flawless, and attend to my home and church duties with a cheerful heart and appreciation. Appreciation, that's what I need most of all. Appreciation for God, and my parents, and my brothers and school and . . . I could go on forever . . . I'm so unworthy, so weak and trouble-giving and unworthy!

Oh please, please God, make mom well and I'll never ask for anything more as long as I live. It hurts so bad to know that she is in such misery. Oh dear God, what if that's because someone else is substituting at the pharmacy. I can't stand that thought! But it's possible!

All the relatives are fasting until after the specialists make their diagnosis. Usually fasting is so difficult but this time it's a wonderful feeling bringing the whole family closer together. Aunt Ruth took me in her arms last night and I cried like a kid while she patted my hair. It's a terrible thing but it seems like tragedy brings people closer together, makes them more supportive, more dependent.

I'm so glad I've got you, journal. It's like . . . I don't know, but I guess it's like going to a psychiatrist . . . I can just get rid of all my fears and frustrations, at least dilute them, by writing in you.

January 15

What a day! Can you believe I won All-State Finals Forensic Society? Every word that came out of my mouth was just right! Imagine winning over high school kids, 500 in the first elimination. Me . . . Me . . . a not yet sixteen-year-old snot-nosed kid, winning over those suckers. It was mom's first really big night out and I think I did it mostly for her. She's so special in my life. And it was so special of her to make me homemade bread to celebrate. Man, what a family! I'm going to make President of the National Thespians for them next year or bust!

In some ways I'm kind of like two people, the easy coasting me when I'm not in competition; the precise slugger when I'm on stage.

THE JOYS OF ARGUMENTATIVE SPEAKING

I have told several different people that nothing can be compared to the feeling you have after completely destroying the confidence of a person in himself by 'wiping him out' in debate. Yes, you do have kind of a feeling of achievement (mixed with pity, especially if there are girls and they cry) but the greater joy lies in the fact that you are maybe causing people to think, to react a little and that you are developing an argumentative style, a basic speaking style and an analytical mind. These are the real joys of debate. You can feel yourself becoming better. Then there are the people you meet, many of them pretty cool and some of them sloppy dinks; but on the average, you will be attracted to the cool people and the others will repel or just do nothing.

January 17

Brad's date last night was an octopus. He said he had to fight her off all night. I could hear them scuffling around in the back seat but I thought he was the one making the moves. Judas, isn't that funny, Brad having to protect his virginity by practically slugging the wench. Man, I didn't know Caroline had the hots for him like that, I guess he didn't either or he wouldn't have asked her out. Come to think of it, she and Mela asked *us*. Mela even furnished the car, and actually, come to think of it in more detail, Mela roughed me up more than I did her too. I'm not getting into that all-the-way thing again though. Good little church girls . . . except at the drive-in movies. Ha, if their mothers only knew. I feel like telling them. Brad and Dell are both virgins and they're right! There should be a single standard for both girls and boys, good! Then there's me . . . nonrelevant, nonpredictable . . . ass-headed!

I think for Brad's birthday I'm going to buy him a lock for his zipper when he goes out on dates. Wouldn't that be a laugh. Him opening this present and family all wondering what the hell it was. Man, I've got to think of some way to do that. He may wet his pants before the evening is over . . . but, oh, Judas I wish Dell was here so we could plan it together.

January 25

Isn't it funny how many different kinds of 'love' and 'lust' there are. Dad told me once when I was going with Debbie that I was not in love but just in 'lust.' It seemed sort of nutty then but now I'm beginning to understand because while I have mixed emotions about Barry I know that part of the feeling of security and peace that I have around her is that I know where she stands. 'No handseys!' It really makes for a nice, comfortable relationship. We're 'buds,' someone dependable to study with or go to games and dances with but no fooling around. It's really a fantastic feeling of un-pressure, is that a word?

January 30

Barry's got this little sister who's a mongoloid. At first I felt uncomfortable around her, and always tried to really not see her, but you know she's a sweet kid once you get to know her, even though she drools and she's always got this funny kind of grin on her face. Sometimes I used to have to fight myself to keep from pulling away from her when she came close, but now I'm beginning to *like* her, not just endure her—but really *like* her! She has a kind of innocence and peace and tranquility that none of the rest of us, in the normal sphere of living, even come close to. Like when she cut herself, she didn't cry or scream like Chaddy would have done or curse a little, like Kendall, if mom hadn't been around, would have done. She just looked surprised that anything or anyone could or would hurt her. It was so sweet and gentle I felt like Barry did and wanted to hold her and take the pain away, in fact even take it on myself. I like the way she makes me feel inside. Like I really do care about more than myself! I'm sure she even makes my relationship with Barry better. I wonder how I'd feel though if Barry ever wanted to take her with us to the Mall or something. I know I'd be embarrassed, probably even mad, because I'd know other people would be making fun of her the way I used to do with people that were different. Life is strange. I wonder if I'll ever really understand it. Maybe I should go into psychiatry, but I dunno, all the psychiatrists I've ever known were as cuckoo, and uptight, and had kids as rotten as anybody else. It would be terrible to go into a field that had no concrete answers.

February 1

Can you believe only fourteen more days and I'll be sixteen? *SIXTEEN! SIXTEEN!* I'll have wheels! No more having to have a licensed driver with me. No more sneaking cars—no more feeling guilty . . . I can't bear the wonder of it.

February 15

THIS is the day! I got my driver's license and I wanted to drive completely around the world without stopping, over both the Pacific and the Atlantic oceans and through the Sea of Galilee and every other place I could think of. I did drive to Troy and back all by myself. I didn't even want Barry or Brad with me. It was kind of like something I had always looked forward to that was almost sacred. That's dumb, isn't it? To worship a car. That's almost what it is, though. I cut school. Mom didn't know that, but I think she understands how important a car is in my life, I know dad does. He's been as excited as I about my getting a driver's license. He joked and teased about how none of the streets would be safe anymore and how little old ladies would lock themselves and their kids and their pets indoors when I was at the wheel and stuff, but I'm sure that's just because he understands how important it is to me.

After school I picked up Brad and Barry and we just cruised till time to go to work, stopping only long enough to get a hamburger to eat on the way, and gas; man, gas is expensive! I've *got* to get myself a VW or something I can support. I've got $420 in the bank so it shouldn't be too long before I can pick up some kind of a clunker.

February 19

I guess I've got the neatest parents in the world. Tonight when I was telling them about the little VW I'd seen advertised in the paper and had gone to see they both smiled at each other and said they would make up the difference. Wow! With their $180 and my $420 I'll have *wheels!* Tomorrow during lunch period mom's going to pick me up and take me to the bank, then to pick up *my* car! MY CAR! It's like saying MY WORLD! It's a clean little critter. Green as a little fat toad and just as cute!

February 27

Dad says I'm trying to polish the paint off Toad, but I'm not. I'm just showing him how much I love him. Barry loves him too, she's helped me clean the motor and polish the chrome. He's our little buddy. And our school sticker is practically his shade of green. Isn't that neat?

It's funny how Barry can be so much like Dell. Of course, she'll never take his place! No one ever could.

February 28

Barry's into drama. She keeps telling me how much I'd love it but I don't know—it seems so damned gay and fruity or something . . . being an actor. She wants me to try out for the play they're casting but . . . Judas, I think I'd hate her through all of eternity and beyond if I fell on my ass, even trying out and not getting the part would be an injury to this puffed up but necessary ego of mine that I'm not sure would ever heal.

March 1

Barry was on my case again today. I've got to decide by tomorrow. I thought it would be easier if I tried to put my thoughts on paper, most things are to me, but not this. . . . I know if we both got parts we'd be together more of the time and have another common interest . . . but what if she got a part and I didn't . . . what if I got a part and she didn't? Oh crap . . . no inspirations . . . no answers . . . no decisions.

March 2

It's all these crappy little decisions that drive people bananas. Barry and I are even fighting. Twelve-thirty but I think I'll sneak out and push Toad down the driveway and go for a cruise.

March 3

I've really got life in a bundle! Me . . . Me . . . imagine me! One of the leads and Barry with one of the others . . . Oh we're so neat, so fortunate and neat and talented! But I've never done anything like this before, I wonder if I'll wet my pants half way through the first act. In a way I'm kind of sorry I let Barry talk me into it, acting is so . . . so dependent. It's not like debating where you can change your strategy and your style and timing and pressure, it's . . . I guess I'll just have to wait and see what it is. At least it's only two days till we start rehearsal, then I'll know. Man, I hope it won't be a bummer.

May 30

ACTING . . . ACTING . . . ACTING . . . It's the most exciting thing that has ever happened to me. It's like debating, only somehow more fulfilling. . . . It's like being someone else—or like being *me* as a new form of existence. It turns me on, and on, and on, and on.

THE JOYS OF THE THEATER

You're thinking, what would he do, what would he think, how would he react? You start pulling. Pulling out the little packaged thought, feelings and emotions that will make you that character. Then the other people, so talented, so quiet and caring but so open and loud and emotional. Everyone can feel the vibrations, the audience is restless, the people want a show. They paid money to sit in the auditorium and watch the fantasy of the emotions, both real (method) and unreal (technique). Then (the curtain opens), everyone smiles and some shake a little. The first words are said, the first jokes are cracked and the audience laughs and at the end (the time goes so fast, you're so involved in being that person that you live in a fantasy that included time as fast time; the faces in the audience, the people, all make the time go fast), at the end, the applause picks you up from the stage, lifts you into a different world and you don't come back till the next morning. The chills, the smiles, the embraces, the smell of cold cream and pancake, the tears, the cheers, the smell of perspiration, the running jumps in the hall, the 'how was I?' and 'how did it go?' The 'great

show's' and the 'hey you guys were good's.' That
is the reward, the joy in the theater is the theater
and what it stands for. The stage, a fantasy, and
for just those moments you on that stage with God
knows how many faces looking at you.

June 1

The let-down is incredible! I was upped on school, debating, drama, Barry and Brad. Now they're all gone.
Barry and Brad's folks both took their vacation right
after school was out. Dad wants to let his employees
go first, good old dad, poor old us.

Working is a bore, maybe I could get something else,
but what? Every other job I could hold would be just
as boring as the one I've got. Why can't I be an astro-
naut or an oceanographer or a brain surgeon, just for
the summer? I'm a pea-brain that lives on wishes and
fantasy and doesn't know his ass from his head, that's
why!

June 4

Oh agony, pain, torture . . . torment . . . carelessness
. . . drunken driving. I wrecked little Toad. Almost
totaled him. Dad won't even talk to me about him. Oh
crap, if he'd just talk . . . but like he says, 'What is
there to say?' I was drunk, I was out with Lucy Loose
Legs. . . . I was a fool, an idiot and a nincompoop. I
know better.

Dad didn't say a thing about grounding me. I guess
he knows I couldn't be any more hurt. In a way I wish
he had inflicted some kind of punishment, at least then

I could have put some of the blame on him, hated him a little more and myself a little less, shared the blame, put it on somebody, anybody. The insiders, the outsiders. Oh Judas, what am I going to do?

June 6

Went out with Carl and Nelson, they're both into Astra baloney. I was so damned lonely. There's nobody but nobody left in this screwed-up little berg. Everybody took off for vacation as soon as school was out like rats leaving a sinking ship. Everybody but us! Carl and Nelson are such nerds! I should be able to understand how they are curious and intrigued by all that supernatural crap, because I've been through it. Judas, I'll keep what I've got, thank you. They can both go kiss a cactus.

June 7

Carl has an Ouija board at his house. It's really creepy how these things work. It answered questions about me and Debbie and about me and Pete that nobody in the whole world could have known except me. It's funny but the bloody thing won't work for Nelson. It just plain doesn't move or when it does move doesn't make sense. I asked it about my auwa and it said 'no' and wouldn't move any more the whole night.

We levitated coins and light objects for a while. Carl is better than I am. Nelson just keeps trying. He's really kind of scared. I'm not anymore because now I'm just investigating in a scientific way. There has to be some explanation of these powers that we can't understand. It must be kind of like an electric or magnetic force that we all possess but just don't do anything about.

Refusing to check into this kind of phenomena is kind of like disregarding knowledge. It does exist. I cannot deny that it exists.

I can see a red aura around Carl. Nelson has a gray one that floats off almost cloudlike from him. I really have to concentrate to see them now. I guess even this type of skill like all others is lost with lack of use.

June 8

I've had a real strange feeling since Carl and Nelson left. When we were using our Astra expertise Kendall came running into my room crying. He was having bad dreams of things he couldn't explain. A few minutes later Chaddy toddled in all sleepy eyed and scared. He had felt the same vibes or whatever. I had to leave both their lights on to get them to go back to sleep. I was glad mom and dad weren't home.

A while later when we were talking to the Ouija board Chaddy came in again. I know he'd never seen an Ouija board before because I hadn't until I saw Pete's at the Pine Boys' School; anyway Chad pulled away from it like it was poison and said he hated it. Isn't that hard to comprehend? I wonder if Chad could feel its psychic forces? Being so young naturally he couldn't understand them, or maybe he's just too young to handle them so he feels afraid. I wish I could talk to dad about these things but I'm sure he'd try to get me to drop the whole research project I've decided to do about the occult. I can't do that! The occult thing is growing so fast it has to have something. In fact, I know it has something—I've seen and used its powers! If I find it's wrong or does evil, after I do my research, I'll get dad to help me instigate a drive against it.

June 9

I tried to talk to Pete at the Pine Boys' School but whoever answered the phone was very curt to me when he found out what I wanted; he wouldn't give me any information at all, just said Pete had left and that they didn't have any forwarding address, then Bang—he hung up.

I was so curious I waited a couple of hours then called back and asked for Dave. Everybody knew he'd be there for a long time because he was a ward of the court and considered violent and dangerous, but he was into the supernatural and knew Pete well. Sure enough Dave finally came to the horn. After the initial shit I asked him about Pete and his voice lowered. He said he couldn't talk. I gave him my address and he promised to write right then. I can't wait for the mail tomorrow, or will it take till the next day?

June 11

Dave's letter has about done me in. I'm not surprised that Pete was a fruit, but raping a little ten-year-old boy in the broom closet? Man, what kind of a weirdo is that? And hurting him enough so they had to take him to the infirmary? Dave said he'd have killed Pete if he hadn't cut-out before the kid was found.

I wonder how long it would have been before Pete put the move on me? Dave said he got to no telling how many kids with promises or bribes or just gentle offers of friendship and acceptance. Lots of kids need that so badly they would do almost anything to get it from almost anyone. Judas, just thinking about it makes me sick to my stomach, and I thought Pete was *soooooo* neat! I wonder if he was using PCP or something?

June 12

I think I'll ask the folks if I can visit Dell in Las Vegas if Mr. Thomas will give me time off at the store.

June 14

Wow! Leaving in two days. Everything went so smooth I can't believe it. In a way I'm sorry to go because both Brad and Barry will be home right after I leave. But it will be super neat to see old Dell again. We haven't written but he was so excited when I got him on the phone he about broke my eardrum with his scream.

I feel rotten that I can't take Toad down but it's going to be some months before I get the bread to repair his wounds. Man, Dell would have loved him so much and we would have had such fun, but at least Dell says his dad lets him drive an old Apache truck at night after work. He also said maybe his dad would let me work on one of the jobs. They really make money! Maybe if I stayed the whole summer I could have Toad all repaired when school started. Wouldn't that be a splash in the sky?

Later—I'm glad I ate my dinner before I got Kurt's phone call cause now I'm sick again. He said he'd heard I needed Koodo and that he couldn't talk on the phone but that I'd get his letter tomorrow. Judas, I didn't want to hear from him. I don't want any more to do with that mess of mixed ups. I'm sick of the whole thing! I just want to get to Las Vegas with Dell.

June 15

Got this crazy letter from Kurt, the young nutso whose dad was the electrician at the Pine Boys' School. Man, am I happy I'm leaving tomorrow! That whole bunch of weirds are short a few bricks of a full load, short a few cards of a full deck, short a few ounces of a full pound, short an inch or two of a full foot, in short—shorted out a little in the brain . . .

June 16

I can't get over Kurt's crazy letter. How did he know Barry had been trying to get me to become a Presbyterian, and that a couple of times I'd thought about it. *Nobody knew about that! I didn't even write that thought down, it just came into my mind. And how did he know about my wishing someone would move to Apple Hill with a Karma similar to mine?* AND THAT I'd been thinking about Deb again? Was it ESP? Was it Cosmic Consciousness? I don't understand, but neither can I deny that there are powers existent here on this planet that science hasn't yet investigated. Maybe that is *my calling,* maybe it's up to me, without bias or malice, to explore these concepts, catalogue them, seriously consider them and present them to some group at some university that can take on from there. I know certain departments are experimenting with ESP and parapsychology. I might be able to give them much helpful information. Well, I don't have to worry about any of that far-out stuff now since I'm leaving for Las Vegas on the afternoon bus. I'm excited! Man, I'm excited! It's been such a dull nothing summer so far. I need you, Dell. You'll never know how much I need you to get my act together. Maybe I'll just forget the whole scene. When school starts again I'll be so busy with Toad, and scholastically, and in the theater and forensics there won't be any time left for that kind of crap anyway.

June 17

I'm so glad I brought you to L.V. with me, Journal. I almost didn't until I saw that built-in lock on the little foot locker. Can you believe that Dell is into the occult here? Man, that was the biggest blow to my head in the world. Judas, I didn't know O was underground in most schools. It's scary. I want to get Dell the hell out! HE can't go into it like I can, undetached and scientifically.

Dell's dad says he has a job for me for the rest of the summer and Hallelujah, I'll be making twice what I made at home. Little Toad will love that. It will assure him that he can come out of retirement when school starts, or maybe I'll just mail my paychecks home to dad and let him start having the work done on old Toad. Judas, that makes me happy, but the other, Dell into all the kinky business. I don't know if I can handle that, but I guess I can. I have to! As long as I can stay detached I'm all right, I must keep reinforcing that thought. But it sure knocks the hell out of what I thought it would be down here. All the laughs and pranks and fun. Dell can be so serious and morbid when he talks about O. Crap, maybe tomorrow will be different, and besides Dell's brother, Kim, is yelling at me to turn out the light. All three of us have to sleep in one room.

June 18

I feel like a man! Working on a big construction job just like all the other men. Of course I'm just a gopher but that's cool. I can dig everything about this business,

hauling the nails and lumber, picking up, cleaning up
. . . GETTING MY PAY CHECK AT THE END OF
THE WEEK! It's exciting!

Some of the guys have got mouths like toilets, but I
guess that's how it is in the construction business.

This is a big house but with Dell and me and his
Mom and Dad and his five brothers and sisters and his
old aunt, man, it's a mess, a noisy, do without, messy
mess.

Tomorrow Dell's dad is going to pile us all into his
van and take us to Hoover Dam; that's going to be exciting. I remember studying about the dam in geography and I just read about it again in a brochure they've
got here.

Imagine, 726 feet high, one of the highest dams in
the world, and we get to go down inside it in an elevator. Lake Mead is one of the largest man-made bodies of water in the world. I don't know what Los
Angeles and the rest of that area would do without it.
It certainly couldn't have expanded like it has.

June 19, 1:30 A.M.—*Just past June 18!*
The trip to Lake Mead was a disaster! Fighting, quar-
reling, snot-nosed kids whining for everything in sight
and if one kid wanted something or to do something,
the others didn't and vice versa. Judas, what a madhouse, and Dell's mother is a bitch, she yells all the
time. But then I guess I'd yell too with all those brats
acting like animals in a zoo, and living temporarily in
someone else's house and in such a crummy district.
I'm glad tomorrow, or today, is Sunday. I never thought
I'd be glad to go to Sunday school. It's always been an
I-had-to-do-it thing, at least the last year or two. Last

September I remember I told my dad he was taking away my free agency by making me go and he said, 'Oh no, I'm not taking away your free agency, you still have a right to choose. You can go either willingly or unwillingly.' Isn't it strange that now, sitting at the kitchen table away from all the confusion and rabble, I feel a need to go. Maybe I just miss my parents, and little Chaddy and Kendall. I've never been away from home much except with the scouts and the nightmare at the Pine Boys' school. I really do miss my family. I wonder if I'll feel this way when I'm grown up and married or away at college. Actually I don't care if I do because it's a nice warm belonging feeling even if it hurts.

> I miss you now that I am here
> And you are there.
> I miss the way you look
> The way you care
> I wanted oh so very much
> To get away
> Now every single day I stay
> I miss you more
> And love you more
> And need you more.

3:45 P.M.

Everyone is taking their Sunday afternoon nap except the little kids who are buzzing around somewhere. I'm embarrassed I enjoyed our Sunday school class so much. The teacher was talking about the miracle of forgiveness and it was like he was talking to me alone. Man, I really do need to consider that concept. Every rotten thing I've ever done in my life, and that's a pile, keeps cropping up in my mind to make me feel guilty, unworthy, less-than-everybody-else in existence. I pretend I've got lots of confidence and I'm a big jock and like that but deep inside I'm a frightened, insecure, can't-make-it-failure.

I must forgive myself for all the rotten things I've done. I know . . . I REALLY KNOW that God has forgiven me. He is so kind and loving and considerate and ever-supportive. If I loved myself as much as I love Him, I could forgive myself completely too, couldn't I? *Jesus said the first and greatest commandment was to love the Lord with all my heart and strength, and that the second was 'like unto it,' I should love my neighbor as myself.* I really have got to start working at loving myself . . . reverencing myself . . . I am God's child, in God's image! And there is no way I can be a good neighbor, or even completely love God until first I've learned to love myself. O.K. neat old great self, let's get this book locked back in the foot locker so we can take a nap too and then get up and help Dell's mom fix a bite before we go to church. That will be being a good neighbor to her and she really needs it with all this mob to control as well as feed and clothe and clean up after. She's a special, special lady to even let me stay here with them when they're in such a hassle. I am going to be more appreciative and more helpful. She's neat . . . but I sure miss mom's bread! I wonder if I can send her an ESP message to send some.

June 20

I worked just part of a week but I still got the old check home to dad to start fixing up Toad. I only kept out ten dollars which is really going to keep me on a string,

since Dell and me have to pay for gas and stuff as well
as an occasional hamburger. I'm glad Dell isn't involved with chicks. They're too expensive! Even when
they go dutch.

We're going to another O meeting tonight. I wish we
weren't, but . . .

Working is fun but it is sooooo hot. Man, sometimes
I pick up a hammer or something by the metal end and
it about takes the skin off my hand. Everybody just
works in their pants and I'm so sunburned I look like a
tomato but Dell said he did the same thing when he
first started, then he peeled and now he's brown, brown,
brown, and looks great. He's also growing a pretty good
mustache; I'm trying but it looks like the moths have
been in it. Like a dirty, fuzzy, little, barely visible cat-
erpillar on my lip. I'll give it another week, maybe by
then I'll get over looking like I've got the mange. Once
our cat Hamlet got the mange and looked in spots just
exactly like my lip does. Oh crap, I want so much to
be macho . . . macho with three hairs on my chest and
thirteen under my arms? Girls seem to think I'm pretty
neat looking though, but then most of them have got
the hots for anything that's male.

Oh hell, I'm upset about tonight, and in a way,
scared. Why? Maybe it's possible that, like they say in
O, sacred secrets *have* been passed down from the ancients to the chosen few! Am I being a hypocrite and
unworthy to go into their research? I'm so cynical, so
hypocritical. Just like I accuse everybody else of being.
I must try to be fair, open-minded and unbiased, a
seeker of wisdom and truth.

I know the crystal ball works. Is it like the seer stone
the Bible mentions? I've seen shadows in it myself.
Nothing real yet but that's not necessarily the ball's

fault. It's most probably because I haven't yet attuned myself . . . like the auras and the auwa. *I* had to put forth the effort. *I* had to learn the principles and use them. I must go into this research like a professional! I can and I will! Another depth, another principle, another form of power long held from men because of their disbelief and unwillingness to open up their minds. Maybe I . . . I . . . I will be the instrument through which these great sources, new to us yet well known to the ancients, are channeled to the learned and the caring who want to use them, along with electricity and atomic power and the other wonders found in the last century or so.

Or am I just trying to give myself a snow job?

June 21

Dell's Dayan is unbelievable. At first I thought he was weird and fakey. Then he looked in the ball and told me things about myself that even Dell couldn't have told him. I felt cold chills ripple up and down my back. He told me he would start the mark of Christ in the palms of my hands and the heat that generated *only there* became unbearable. I tried to convince myself that he had just put that thought in my mind and I was doing it myself, but then he told me I must also hang on my own cross. *Absolutely, thoroughly and completely against my will I walked* over to a huge neon flickering cross on one wall and stood before it. The pain was excruciating. The tears streamed down my face, tasted salty in my mouth, and wet the front of my shirt. I could only moan for them to set me free.

No one was touching me! No thing was touching me! And yet I could feel pain in my hands and feet that I could not endure. Was it an electric current from the neon cross? After what seemed forever I felt a torturous thrust in my side that made me scream then took my breath away. The force was invisible and I wondered if they were using some kind of laser beam. As I was trying to rationalize myself out of the maze the pain became so great that I felt myself go limp, my head fall to my shoulder. It was over.

When I awoke Dell and eleven others were anointing my body with oil and chanting together over me. I felt a kind of peace and relaxation that I had never felt before. The only thing that even compares with it was one time in a dentist's chair when he had been giving me nitrous gas and was called to the phone. I wonder if somehow they had given me nitrous. Did they have a hidden tank somewhere? Was it somehow piped into the whole room?

The Dayan was leaning over me, "We have another doubting Thomas, yes?"

I closed my eyes. The feeling was too great not to enjoy. It's 4 A.M. and I still can't comprehend or understand what happened. We are sworn to secrecy on a blood and death oath, but I think of myself sort of as a spy among the enemy or a seeker of truth that is above restrictions. Am I right? Oh God, I wish I had never gotten into this. Pete said, and now the new Dayan confirms, that what I'm learning is just an extension of Christianity, just the secrets that were known by the ancients at the time of the first peopling of his world. All the secrets and powers that were given from Adam on down as man was able to receive them.

I better get to bed or I'll never be able to do my work tomorrow, I feel so tired—not tired, exhausted, drained, pooped, consumed. Maybe I'll wake up and find it all hasn't happened. Who am I to try to be the bridge between two worlds? Me, the weak one that can't even control my own destiny.

Oh Judas, I'm confused.

June 22

It's hard to put into words what's happening. I feel so stupid and as I read the words back they sound like I'm some kind of a psycho or something. I must constantly remind myself:

> Great concepts
> Start small
> Grow tall.
> The tiny acorn
> Grows into a tree.
> I like the acorn
> Shiiiiiiiiit.
> Am a nut.

Dell and I talked to our Dayan till two thirty tonight or today or whatever. He really convinced me they're not like the crazy Moonies who are trying to say *he's* the Messiah. They're just *an extension* of what good we already believe. They don't want to take that away from us, indeed they just want us to build on what we already have, enlarge and enlighten our own souls, develop and estimate our own spiritual growth from where we are! He says Pete's deplorable actions put a restriction on my aura and auwa, rather I put it on myself, because of him. So I cannot expand beyond a certain point until I lift that restriction and let my good vibrations flow out to encircle the world. He really makes that seem both possible and plausible. He used the simile that if the world were covered with calm water and I threw in one little stone those ripples would go out and out until they encompassed the whole body. I believe that in a sense, also, that people can feel my anger or my love, that my vibrations do touch them, do warm them or cool them, do give them happiness or detract from that happiness. I also believe like he says that life is made up of negative and positive currents like electricity, positive thoughts and actions triggering off positive power for good. Negative thoughts and actions doing the opposite. They are true principles. But I don't know . . .

Maybe I'm not in enough or out enough.

Dell says he's happy and he religiously goes through his rituals in the bathroom every night, even though sometimes he's interrupted a hundred times or more before he's through. Man, this is really a madhouse. It would be hard to have any kind of personal discipline here, and yet both the girls take piano lessons and Mike practices trombone and Kim practices saxophone. I'm glad I didn't bring my guitar. We couldn't stand any more music! That's music?

July 30

I'm grateful for this big old tree behind the house closed in by shrubs. It's the only place where anyone can have privacy. I'm surprised that all the others haven't found it. Oh the kids use it for a hideout sometimes but most of the time it's forsaken, forgotten, the only place of peace and quiet in the whole area. Is it possible that other people don't need a quiet place for peace and meditation like I do? Am I the only one who has to ponder over things, think them out, try to find answers? Am I the only one that in trying to organize thoughts only makes them more unfathomable, more debilitating, more confusing?

I felt so much more secure when I was satisfied with my little world as it was, now the more powers I receive the more answers I need. I can do things that are only done in science fiction! These principles *do work!* The Ouija board told me my dad would call tonight, and that it would be good news. I can't wait.

August 1

Sure enough dad did call last night and it was not only good news but fantastic! The family is going to drive to Vermont, leaving next week, coming back just in time for school. Dad's going to take off three weeks, can you believe that? When I first heard it I thought the world would cave in. Three weeks! Wow! It will be kind of a historic trek, one I've always wanted to go on and now it's here! Dad and mom and the kids were all talking at one time on both extensions so I'm sure I didn't get much straight, but at least I know I'll take the bus from here on Saturday and we'll leave Apple Hill on Monday.

AFTER DINNER

John came over to the job during his lunch break and told me to be careful, that the Ouija had said I was in danger.

For a few minutes it shook me up then I decided that I wasn't superstitious and all that stuff so I just went about my business but I guess his message had somehow subconsciously made me alert because the cement bucket came off the crane just before closing time and that mother missed me by two inches. If I hadn't jumped and rolled away when I felt some negative power coming at me I'd have been smashed flat as a pancake. As it was I was completely covered with cement, *I mean completely!* They had to dig me out, clean me off with the firehose and take me to the emergency clinic, in a state of mild shock. I didn't tell anybody but Dell about the warning from John, but man, it's really got my hair on end. I suppose I should be grateful for this special power of discernment that I, or John, had been given. I'm thankful that I am one of the few.

John says he's from Atlantis. I couldn't have swallowed that a year ago, in fact I remember in a note one time Tim said he was ruler of Atlantis. I wonder whatever happened to Tim. All this stuff seemed then like garbage to me. I really can't comprehend it now—but it does work! Judas, I wish I knew how it really works! Will I ever? Do I want to? Shall I give up my project? I think I will. Yeah, I think I will.

I can't feel good about it on a gut level. Maybe it's me . . . I guess it is me, but nevertheless, I'm going to play sick till Saturday so I won't have to expose myself to any more stuff I can't dig.

It must have been 114 degrees on the job today. The sweat dried on us before it even got out of our pores, leaving everybody feeling like they had a coating of salt on their bodies. Just as we were getting ready to quit Big Buck took a handful of water from the cooler and splashed it on Dell's dad, he took the cupful he was drinking and threw it back, and before anyone knew what had happened we were all in a water fight to end all water fights. We started with cups and buckets and hats full of water and ended up with two firehoses. Man,

I never dreamed the power those things had, they just swashed us across the ground like we were skating, on our butts, that is. Everybody laughed and screamed until they were hoarse. It was a fantastic kind of farewell for me although none of them knew that's what it was.

I got all the skin torn off my elbow and my wrist as I was sloshed first in one direction and then in the other by the two firehoses. Like in the regular army the older guys kept me and Dell and another kid out in the main line of fire, they kind of playing it safe in the rear. Anyway it was fun, although the language was about as salty as I've ever heard.

After the water fight me and Dell went to a semi-bar with Ted and Big Buck and Rod and Hank. Of course, Dell's dad didn't know about that. They mixed whiskey with our 7-Up and told us stories about nude wrestling matches, between men and women and all kinds of horny degenerate stuff.

It's a strange thing about Vegas. There's the raunchy, gambling, Mafia, adult XXX-rated everything side, and then there's the residential area where the straights live. Dell's aunt told me there are more churches per permanent resident there than in most cities and towns in the nation, and that while the wild people are wilder, the straight people are straighter. . . . Life is strange, yeah?

August 2
7:30 P.M.—PLAYING SICK
Man, it's deadly with Dell gone to an O meeting and just the brats around shaking the house off its foundation. We're all so studious in our house, we don't do

that much jumping and running and screaming. We're more likely to be settled down with a book or a project of some sort. Not that we don't fight . . . and fight . . . and fight . . . but even that's kind of loving and I miss it. I guess no one in the world ever really, really belongs except in their own God-given, precious, supportive, peaceful, caring family.

August 7

I guess I'll jot down some things in this little note book and add them to my journal when I get back from our vacation.

Everybody's asleep and I don't know how they can do it. A strange town, Leadville, Colorado, a strange motel, me in the bathroom curled up on a blanket I dragged in so I could have some privacy.

How can they sleep when it's so exciting! Different places! Different faces. Seeing more of God's beautiful world.

Some day when I'm dad's age I want to travel to Japan and China and Russia, Thailand and Norway, Germany and France, England and Ireland, Australia and the South Seas.

It's so cozy in here between our connecting rooms. I can hear dad snoring and mom breathing softly and Kendall and Chad sniffing and snorting and making other strange, nice, little boy noises. I hope neither one of them ever get their lives as screwed-up as I did mine. But I'm all right now, soft and warm and protected through our remaining forever. Oh dear God, I am blessed to be in this family.

August 11

I love Chicago. Coming into it through the miles of grain fields and barns so big they are like castles, I thought we had come across a new race of people.

In the little towns, they're just like us, complaining about the weather, and the prices too high and the government officials too low. But in the city, man the city, it's so crazy and rough, the wind blowing and the buildings piercing up through the sky making their own ragged peaks, their own Grand Tetons and Rocky Mountains. The people seem hurried, hard and piercing as their buildings. I wouldn't want to live here, but I loved walking down the wild, windswept lake shore fighting to keep each grain of sand and seashell as its own. The birds on the beach seemed as aggressive as the weather and the surroundings. In fact two seagulls started fighting over some bit of debris they had picked up and I swear it sounded like they were both squealing, 'mine, mine, mine.'

The family broke up laughing when I told them what I thought it sounded like but they all agreed.

Maybe next year Brad and Dell and I can take Toad and come back here on our own. Wouldn't it be fun just the three of us crossing the nation? It shouldn't cost too much in Toad and we could take our bedrolls and buy most of our food in markets. We'll have to work on the parents and the cost factors and such when I get back. If we start planning right now it shouldn't be any sweat at all.

August 16

I really had meant to write every day, but at night usually I was pooped . . . pooped . . . double pooped, besides I've categorized everything in my mind. The fantastic mountains around Denver, the quiet rolling-ness of Nebraska and Iowa, Lake Michigan, the unbelievable beauty of upper New York State. I always thought of New York as being like New York City. It isn't! It's quaint and rural and I love it! I sound like a geography freak and I'm not, I didn't even particularly like the subject—but now I'm convinced that if one traveled and got to really know the places instead of just having dumb, dull facts crammed down their throats it might be exciting.

August 20

Tomorrow we start on our homeward trek. I'm glad mom talked dad into bringing us up to Niagara Falls as a climax; I guess next to the Grand Canyon that's the most spectacular thing I've ever seen.

Mom was so cute, almost like a little girl as she had dad get them a room *not connected* with ours. Actually it isn't even in the same wing with ours. Come to think of it I don't know where it is, but that doesn't matter. I'll take the kids walking along the paths by the falls, maybe take a boat ride, man, that would be exciting, riding right under the falls! Then we'll shop at the souvenir stores, have dinner and more sight-seeing. One can't get too much of that here! This whole area defies description. It's magnificent! The roar and pounding of the water, the strength and volume, I'm *really* impressed! We're on the Canada side and everyone says we're a hundred times safer here than on the American side. Isn't that sad! But anyway it's nice for us. I guess we all needed a break from each other, although it's been amazingly tranquil. Chad always did sleep a lot in the car, in fact we have to wake him up to see the things that are special. That makes it great for us who don't particularly have any fondness for his restlessness and his demands when he's awake.

I'm excited now about going to Palmyra and Independence and to see the Amish people. I love that part of our old history.

August 28

Today I'm unpacking my gear and I find you, you little flipper. Where have you been? I looked all over for you. Someday when I have time I'll sort your profound statements from your garbage and make entrances in my journal.

September 6

I, great king of the hill, Jack and Jill (who might fall down before the year, or even the day is over and break my crown), am now completely registered in HIGH SCHOOL! APPLE HILL HIGH SCHOOL, WATCH OUT! DELL, BRAD AND JAY, THE THREE NEPHITES ARE HERE! I wonder if Apple Hill High is ready for us? Are we ready for them? Last year in junior high we were the biggies, this year we're the guppies, but not for long . . . I am out to conquer. School prepare, town prepare, state prepare, county prepare . . . I AM COMING! WE *THREE* ARE COMING!

Old Toad is even spryer than before his accident, hopping along the road like it belonged to him. Man, I was glad to have him back. If he weren't so darn big I'd have him sleep in my bed.

I got every class I wanted with no hassle and the whole set-up seems cool! I dig high school and I'm knocking myself out trying to act grown up and not like some half-assed freshman.

Brad and me and Dell share a locker and it's cool, man, cool!

Barry got big as a cow during the summer and her face has erupted out in pimples like volcanos. In a way the fat makes her look somewhat like her mongoloid sister. I feel sorry for her! She's like a different person. She hardly speaks to me or anyone else. And where she used to sit in the front row and be the first one with her hand up she's now trying to find a dark corner in the room or a crack. I wonder if there's anything I could do . . . or more importantly, would I do it if there was?

Me, old jock Jay, would I be seen with some fat chick with zits? I guess not. . . . Now that a good look at the real me has ruined my day I guess I should go clean mom's car and then go to work. Mr. Simons at the auto parts house was really neat to give me a job. Two nights a week plus Saturdays and two and a half hours each day, plus 15 percent off on parts I bought for Toad. I'll be so loaded I won't be able to carry my money to the bank.

September 18

I'm not so sure about my job being all that good. I want to try out for a play but what about the hours for rehearsal? And in forensics most everything big comes off on Saturday. Guess I'll talk to dad tonight about what he thinks I should do. I can't do it all and I need the money for next summer if Dell and Brad and I go on a trip but. . . . Oh hell, sometimes life is really the squirts.

I think I could get on the second string in basketball, Dell and Brad are both trying out, but where to find the hours? I know dad is going to tell me I have to compromise somewhere. But I don't want to compromise! I want all that life has to offer, and I want it on a golden plate with my name engraved. Not really.

Gotta go to work.

LATER

Dad helped me get my life organized. It was really neat. We sat up and talked till almost two A.M. I need the exercise so I'm going out for basketball. I know I'll never make the first string but that's not the main thing in my life like it is for Dell. Besides our tenth grade team isn't that big a deal. Also I decided to give up the theater this semester and keep debating because debating can help me in any profession I decide to go into and is much more mind expanding and demanding. An actor does other people's things, a debater does his own thing, planning, creating and making it work. Yeah, dad is right. His advice was good and I feel much more together, like I know where I'm at and where I'm going, than I have since the day school started.

September 20

Well, things are looking up! Yes, things may be getting better. I might be finding someone 'to see.' Yeah, things are looking up. I just might ask her to the debate party if things go right. Well, there are times, there certainly are times . . .

The vibrations have struck home—someone grown-

up, someone of my kind. Someone real. An individual,
an understanding ear, a seeing eye, an open mind. Living, breathing, walking, talking, listening, loving,
holding.

September 21

The vibrations were right. The time was right. I had
lunch with Tina. Man, she is so cool looking she made
little choking feelings come into my throat when I
looked at her. I've never seen eyes like hers, they are
any color she wants them to be, if she wears gray they
are gray, if she wears blue they are blue, the same with
green, purple, lilac or any soft color. Sometimes, she
says, they're almost yellow if she wears certain rusts or
light orange.

Tina didn't go to our junior high but I'd seen her
around the last couple of years. No one could ever pass
Tina and not remember her. She tried to tease me and
tell me I didn't, but I did of course. She swears she
remembers me from the first football game we ever had
with their school, but I don't know, chicks try to make
guys feel good.

September 22

I asked Tina to the debate party and she said she was
just praying I'd ask her. It was so neat. Sort of like we
belong together. We feel good and easy.

September 23

Tina's parents won't let boys come by. She's been
through her 'dumb days' too. She says her folks are

JAY'S JOURNAL

very strict now, and I'm glad! That makes me feel safe too. Of course I'd never admit that to anyone or even say it out loud.

Tina's running for school vice-president, that's kind of a biggie for a freshman but I guess she knows where her head is. I'm giving her a lot of help and so are Brad and Dell. Man, it's going to take every spare minute any of us have got because we've got a big program laid out.

September 23

Carla, the girl Tina is running against is really a turkey-tail. She's using slanderous kind of garbage, anything she can, and cutting Tina because she's a freshman, like she's a retard. Actually Tina's had an outstanding grade average. We are going to show that tomorrow by putting up a big thermometer by the front door at school showing both their grade averages from first grade. It's going to be a low blow for Carla because Tina's averages are higher than hers! I don't know how Dell ever got Carla's grades. He must have a friend in the office. I didn't ask. It's better not to know some things.

September 24

Tina won! It was almost as exciting as when I win myself. It was funny though, that little cat didn't seem one bit surprised. She had said all along that she would win. At times I had been a little bit worried about what would happen if she didn't, after all, nothing in the competitive area is a 100 percent sure cinch, but anyway, she accepted winning like it had been assured, always been hers.

After I got in bed and tried to get the tension out of my own body I started laughing. I'd been more pressured about the whole thing than she had. I even suspect both Dell and Brad had too.

Man, girls are different. Different and nice!

September 25

High school is a blast. Lots more happening than in junior high. I try to pretend I'm BMOC but I can't get over the bottles of booze in lockers and the pot that's passed around and the pills. It's like the adult population is blind or they really don't care. Don, who has the locker next to us, is getting himself a snort every time I come to change books or something. He must come between every class. I don't know what to do about it, but it hurts me. I've known Don since we were cub scouts together in about the second or third grade or whatever. Man, I'd hate to see him become an alcoholic at sixteen, or maybe he is one already. If so, he deserves and needs help. Why the hell doesn't somebody help? Why the hell doesn't somebody care?

And the kids down at the end of the hall popping pills like popcorn, that makes me so damned mad I want to run for student government and control it from the inside if no one will do anything about controlling it from the outs. Tina's going to try to do something in that area when she gets going in her office.

Maybe I can get some assembly debates set up about drug use and abuse. I tried that once last year and the faculty got uptight as hell. They're so afraid someone is going to say something good about doping that they won't even accept the fact that doping *is good*, that it's fun and exciting! *It's the results that are bad!* It's like they are willing only to see their side and the kids are just as tunnel visioned about seeing theirs. I wonder where this thing will ever end? The blind wanting other people to be blind in that area too! Man, it freaks me out—the stupidity, the waste, the hypocrisy, on both sides. . . . We won't listen. We won't learn! Not only wanting to be blind but deaf. I think I'll talk to the principal tomorrow and see if we can together work up some kind of a program for self-help.

I lie here waiting for Tina's call like it controls the world. Her parents really are strict! *Especially about me!* So she calls me after they are in bed. People would think we were bananas. Us both putting our alarm clocks under our pillows and waking up at 2 A.M. so I can catch her phone call on the first ring. It doesn't seem to bother our sleep though. In fact I think we both sleep better after we've hashed out our problems and things. We're really both on the same wave length . . . have similar auwas . . . oh crap, what made me think of that.

September 26

I can't believe this! Tina's into O too! I say it's a surprise and yet in my heart I really think I've known for some time. When she was so sure of herself about the election . . . and, I don't know, I guess just a couple of little things she's said. I don't know how to lay it on Dell and Brad! We all made a sacred pact to play it cool till Christmas when we were going to have another evaluation in our lives. No booze, no drugs, no sex, no occult! Now this dumped in my lap. Oh crap. . . . I want to go running back to daddy, crying that I've got another problem I can't handle.

September 27

Tina is really strange. She's so cool and loose about most things but when she's talking O she becomes tense and serious as another person, a nine-million-year-old ancient that seems to have all the answers for everything.

Her folks were away for the evening so I went over to her house. She has a beautiful little chest in her room. It's got drawers for jewelry and scarves and stuff, looks mostly like other little what-not pieces, except that it has a secret compartment that opens in the back; in fact the whole back comes out and one sees that actually the drawers in the front are dummies, only go half way through. In this secret part, she's got an Ouija board, a crystal ball, little jars of herbs, lots of Cosmic Consciousness and Rosicrucian stuff about the mastery of life, and of course all the Astra junk. Besides that she's got garbage I've never even heard about like the voodoo wanga she said was mine that she just keeps for me. It's kind of a weird little gismo made in Haiti, the land of voodoo. It's supposed to bring wealth, love, health and good or bad luck.

It was a spooky but fun night, sort of reminded me of the old Halloween parties I went to when I was a kid. Tina and I sat on the floor with a candle between us. In a very low, muted voice she told me how, in the dark evening in the hills of Haiti, the drums begin to throb in the warm night air and the Houngan priests conducted sacred secret ceremonies requesting favors from Ibo, Damballah and other gods. It was like we were there almost. Slivery shaky shadows from the candle wobbled on the walls and curtains as she leaned over and placed the wanga in my hands. Tina said that sometimes wangas were advertised in the *National En-*

quirer and other magazines, but without the knowledge to know how to use them it was sort of like giving a baby electricity when he didn't have the instructions or wasn't smart enough to turn on the switch.

I took the wanga in my hands and felt a strange sensation . . . curiosity mixed with repulsion.

Tina asked me to work through its powers to bend a bobby pin she had placed beside the candle. I felt stupid and couldn't make myself do it. I said I'd pass.

Ignoring my negativeness she began to chant and concentrate herself. Slowly the bobby pin straightened itself from a tight U to a loose, barely bent one.

After a while I relaxed and we levitated a few coins. For me it's physically and emotionally harder than lifting the heaviest weight possible. Tina says it gets easier with time and practice. I hope so. Tonight I sweated like I'd played center through a whole basketball game, just to get two measly little coins four inches off the floor. The bobby pin is the same principle.

Then we messed around for a while with the Ouija board and the crystal ball. Tina said they had both told her emphatically that she was going to win the election, that's why she had never had any question.

What's the difference between what we were doing and faith? The church teaches faith! It's the *'secret combination'* bit that scares me. I can understand why it has to be secret because the scoffing of the unbeliever will dilute its power and yet . . . Oh crap, it's so confusing. Tina is trying to convince me that it seems confusing because I'm just beginning to see that these, unknown to most people, powers work and I don't know yet how they work. I wonder if she's right and it will all be very simple once I understand the principles?

It seems kind of childish and immature of me not to

at least give the whole concept a chance. I know faith works! I've personally seen it heal the sick and other things. God said faith can literally move mountains. I believe that! I can't understand it, but I literally know *both* these strange but uncomprehended power sources work! Or are they both extensions of one?

September 28

Tina's mother thinks she went to a school function. Actually we went to this queer old lady's house who has powers I still can't believe. She actually levitated *me!* I know I didn't just think it because I was very careful not to eat or drink anything. Again, could there possibly be something piped into the air? That's the only explanation other than that it really happened.

We took turns concentrating our group powers on one person and it was amazing how we could make that person feel a sensation that he/she didn't know we had chosen for him/her.

When it was my turn to go into another room, I really strained to hear something but I couldn't. It was like they weren't even whispering as they made their decision. When I got back in the group I sat again in the yoga position like the others and waited; in a few minutes I literally could feel heat waves striking my body. It was like squatting in front of a fireplace and having someone pile Christmas tree branches, or something highly flammable, on the fire. Sweat began to run from my hairline down my face. I tried to fight the power, set up a defense, block it out, but I couldn't. At last when I thought I was going to explode like a pressure cooker I gave up and admitted that I could feel it. . . . Feel it? Judas, it almost cooked me alive. I wonder if their power, or faith or whatever, really could have cooked me . . . killed me?

Wow! This has been my first encounter with voodoo. Who would ever have dreamed that I, the egghead, would become involved in the primitive, the superstitious . . . THE TRUE! It does work. They don't need pins and all the stuff you see on TV and in movies. No, they just need controlled cosmic *mind power*. Once I read about the power of a single atom. We are all composed of atoms, most of us just don't know how to harness their amazingness. The first chance I get I'm going to the university—as well as the public library—and see how much research has been done regarding voodoo and other unknown powers.

It's beginning to scare me less and intrigue me more, and it's easier to stay detached than I thought it would be! A thorough scientific study really must be made of these phenomena.

September 29

This afternoon, after church, Tina said she was going to a girl friend's and we went up the canyon. She had her Ouija board tucked away in her big school bag and we sat under the trees in a little grove and asked it questions about life. At first I felt little rushes of uncomfortableness, but they passed, and we asked about school and sports and my job and our families and everything we could think of.

Then we just stretched out and both took a nap. The yellow leaves that completely covered the ground were like a soft comforter, and the fragrance of the wild shrubs around and the gentle plop plopping of the water over rocks made us feel like two children out of a fairy tale. Old Toad was the good green dragon guarding us and we were safe . . . life was pleasing, fulfilling and at ease.

Did problems and pressures, angers and hurts really exist? Not in our world! I remember thinking all kinds of beautiful thoughts like that while we hung on the fringe of sleep. In fact, I held back not wanting to let go.

What can I say? We communicate, we express, we interact, we feel, we happen. We happen! We (I) can dig it. It just is there. Good vibrations. We lean on each other. It doesn't need reminder, or force of lies or encouragement, it just happens. I am joyful.

September 30

Tina has become part of my life! We cut assembly and lunch and drove up River Dell. She feels as I do that our auwas have merged. That we are one. At her insistence, I am going to include her in my rituals each night as she has included me in hers for some time. She wants me to be one with her in all things, but I'm still holding back about O . . . I didn't say so but I know she can feel it for we can now send ESP messages to each other even though we are in different classes or at home. It's a phenomenon but not one of the powers that are completely foreign to me because I see my parents and other people who have married for long periods and are very close, and they often finish sentences for each other or say 'I know' or something long before any of the rest of us know what's coming off.

I sit here at my desk thinking how important Tina is in my life, how I love her body and her mind and her soul, but I can't be with her completely . . . I can't dedicate myself to her forces, and reject my church completely . . . Everything was fine as long as her thing was an extension of mine, an expansion, but I don't know, if I have to choose . . . will it be her? It's like I'm two people, one who wants to go with her and one who doesn't, and like she's two people and I only want one of them.

Oh sleep,
Why do you wander like a sheep that's lost
And in my time of deepest dark and need of thee
Cannot be found?
Come sleep
And soothe my furrowed head.
Come sleep
And rest with me upon my bed.
Please sleep
Come rescue me
Tis I am lost, not thee.

Tina's parents hate me. It's one constant hassle with them!

October 1
Today Tina gave me this strange note. She said she laid awake last night for hours with my aura torturing hers because of my uncertainty. That my indecision was shattering her.

I feel rotten but I can't change the way I feel. I don't want to! I've got to stay alert and mentally disciplined because I'm turning my paper on the 'Factors Affecting Phagocytosis' in tomorrow as an entry in the medical department of the Science Fair. I can't let anything interfere with that. I won't! Dr. Harten at the hospital research board says I know more about blood than pre-med students starting medical school. I can't give that and everything else I've got going for me up for a few fun trips to Halloween land.

Aw come on, be honest! Actually Aiae has helped me immeasurably with my concentration and mental disciplines. I can literally isolate myself within a mental cocoon while in the midst of the noisiest, most un-hinged environment. *Aiae has to have credit for that.* And some of the other disciplines that I understand and practice I do appreciate, but the whole way . . . *I can't go the whole way.* It's like giving up my free agency! I've been taught all my life that that was one of the greatest principles in life. Oh shit, Tina's making it so difficult!

. . . I'm shattering her reality! . . .

. . . She's shattering my reality . . . and disturbing! . . . I'm practically a mental case!

She says I can't be a complete person without her, nor her without me, that our karma, our auwa . . . our . . . her letter is as mixed up as she is . . . as I am . . . Can we make it together? Man, I love her! I don't want to even try it alone! . . . alone . . . alone . . . The saddest word in the world.

A busted up, confused letter from a busted up, con-fused chick. I didn't want to do that to her. I love her. I don't want to hurt her. I want to soothe her pain . . . make her well again.

October 1, 3:47 A.M.
Actually October 2, but I couldn't sleep, so I prepared my paper on 'Factors Affecting Phagocytosis' and drove

it all the way into the city, and left it in the judge's mailbox. Man, I enjoyed doing that paper. I love mental challenges, mind expanders, things that can't be done or that are difficult to do. Mom and Dad are so proud of me, they're sure I'll win an Air Force Award.

Now I only have to see what the judges say. I can't wait! Man, I hope they like it! What if they hate it? Oh now I'm being paranoid. I've got to make myself go to sleep. I'll be a mess for the game tomorrow as well as for the test in Milner's class.

Good night, good night nice friend. It's important to have someone to tell my troubles to, especially now that I'm so confused about Tina and keeping something from Brad and Dell. That's really hard. I think they suspect. Hell, what do I do? I made a pact . . . a vow . . . a promise . . .

I wonder how I would react to my paper if I were a judge?

October 3

Tina's parents found out about her using the phone at night so they've stopped that and she's got a cold so she's not even in school. In a way it seems good. Dell and Brad and me have been like in the olden days, wandering the halls and spouting off at the chicks, wrestling and playing a little rugby on the lawns when we've got a few minutes and racing around in Toad like he was a sports car. He does his bloody best and we screeched around corners and hung out the windows and threw water balloons. Man, today I felt like I was ten years old again.

October 4

Last night me and Brad and Dell all fell from grace
. . . fell . . . splattered ourselves! After the game Jim
and some of the kids invited us to a kegger up the
canyon so we went, saying all the way up we weren't
going to drink only make out a little with the chicks
but . . . well, we just couldn't resist and once we started
we all tried to outdrink each other, then out pot-smoke
each other. Just as we were getting ready to cut out,
Lyle and Fats came in with some PCP which none of
us had ever tried . . . so . . . not feeling any pain at
this point, we all indulged. Judas, I can't believe that
stuff . . . Just minutes later half the people there were
swinging at each other, even Dell, the peacemaker. I
felt some girl grab my hair and I reached out and clob-
bered her but couldn't beat her off, she was like a wild
animal, just crazy; and I guess I was crazy too.

I saw Brad weaving off through the bushes with some
Loosie Goosie and I remember laughing and thinking
that now I could forget about the little padlock I'd
planned on getting him for his zipper.

October 5

Today in school Tina had Kim slip me a note asking
me to meet her through the block from her house at
midnight. 'Important, urgent, important,' she had put
all around the edge.

It's no trouble to slip out my bedroom window and
roll old Toad down the driveway and let him coast to
the corner before I start the motor, so I did, wondering
a little about Tina because we were having a summer
thunder shower and it was raining and thundering and
lightning like crazy. For a while I thought maybe she

wouldn't come and then she appeared running through the shrubs like some little lost fawn in the mountains.

I tried to talk to her but she seemed cool and detached, directing me to go to a certain house on the outskirts of town that was hidden way back in some trees. At the driveway she told me to stop my motor and turn the lights off and coast in.

Something inside me, all along, had felt kind of squeamish and I wanted *out*, but Tina seemed so intent that she made my sensations seem childish.

She knocked a certain way and the door was opened by a woman as old as my mother and kind of fat. She had on a checked pants suit and looked like every other lady you see in the supermarket, pushing her little old cart. What in hell are we doing here? I asked myself as we were led up a flight of stairs without even introductions.

In a small room at the top of the stairs I stopped wondering. One whole wall of the room was glass like an artist's studio window, and outside the lightning flashed like white neon spears being thrown across the sky. A group of people sat naked around a spurting little candle. Quickly Tina and the woman peeled off their clothes. The old lady's boobs sagging down to her waist and her belly dangling down to her knees. I thought I was going to throw up but I couldn't—I really couldn't move! I could feel the whole group throwing power at me as real as the thunderbolts flashing across the sky, and a strange burning incense filled my nostrils, my throat and my chest. The small room was hazy with the smoke. Detached from my own self, somewhat surprised, I found myself undressing and joining the circle.

I continued to try to fight but soon I was floating

along with the rest. I remember thinking 'What are they burning?' It wasn't hash! What could possibly be that strong? Zombies sat around the flame. Thirteen stoned, ugly, naked zombies.

They went through incantations I had never heard before and did things I, even now, will not let myself believe.

When the storm seemed at its most severe Tina was given a vial filled with a foul smelling, sticky, thick liquid, half of it she drank herself and the other half she passed to me. Like the zombie I was at that point, I drank it; then, as the torrents of rain beat on the window and the lightning shot and exploded through the sky and the thunder roared and banged and crashed through the clouds I hit her and kicked her and mauled her, sex was not enough, I wanted to hurt her! After what seemed hours the drug wore off. The people came back into place in the circle. Panting and groaning, I was led back to mine.

Tina crawled over and gathering blood from her cuts on her fingers she placed it in my mouth. 'Master, Master, Master,' she whispered over and over. I was too groggy to do anything more than swallow.

After eons, someone opened the windows and the doors; a damp, cold blast blew through bringing me partially to my senses. 'Let's get out of this hell hole,' I gagged, hoping I had just had the worst of all bummers.

Tina, whose body someone had patched with big Band-Aids hurriedly slipped on her clothes. 'Let's.'

Nothing was said on the way home. What was there to say? Oh God, I'm ashamed! I know I was drugged but that is still no excuse. Why do they want to do things like that? Why do people want to act like animals? After what happened in the canyon I had vowed never to use angel dust again, but what in the world could they possibly have given us except it? Or worse. Was anything worse? Even the name offended me, was blasphemous! 'Angel dust!' It should be called Devil Dust!

Oh dear God, I've got to do something. I can't let anything like what happened to me happen again or happen to anyone else. I wonder if I wrote an unsigned note to the police department . . . but what could I say? That the place is used by a witch—is a drug drop? Yeah! Yeah, first thing in the morning, before school I'll drive by and get the address and report the house. Oh Judas, how could Tina ever have let me in for anything like that? Let herself become involved? I know she didn't do it willingly. I'm sure she is as heartbroken and humiliated as I am. What am I ever going to say when I see her tomorrow at school . . .

I'm taking three Histaspan. They're only for colds but are supposed to cause drowsiness. I've got to sleep! Sleep is my only way to escape.

October 6

I think I've lost my mind. Tina conducted assembly today like nothing had happened. She had a Band-Aid over one eye and one on her neck, just above her turtleneck sweater, that's all . . . me . . . I'm a basket case. Imagine her accepting the whole thing like . . . Judas, I wanted to stomp right up there on the stage and—no, I didn't, I don't ever want to do anything like that again but . . . Oh crap, I haven't heard one word that was said in any of my classes and she's so cool and together.

I'm sick. Physically, emotionally and, mostly, by far, mostly *spiritually* sick! Oh God, I'm a debased inhuman animal. I hate myself, despise myself, loathe myself.

AFTER DINNER

Judas, it's strange that how when you hate yourself you *hate* everyone else too! I fought with mom and dad at the table and slapped Chad and punched out Kendall when we were supposed to be doing the dishes. Judas, I'm really a Judas! I could have done anything. I did do everything! Could I . . . if I had been living at the time of Christ and been under the influence of drugs have . . . oh dear God, *no* . . . I can't let myself think about things like that or I really will lose my mind!

I wonder if the ancient Roman and Greek civilizations and the people in Sodom and Gomorrah just had orgies when they were all stoned? Was that their excuse too?

10:30 P.M.

Tina came into the store tonight. She looked so tiny and fragile and sad I wanted to take her in my arms and cry . . . with her . . . for her . . . for me . . . for us! She has a big bruise on her cheek and the two Band-Aids that show. Frank asked her what happened. She said she fell down the basement stairs. Frank laughed and said, 'Yeah? I'll bet Jay beat you up.'

I wanted to die. I've never wanted to die so much before in my life, but she just laughed too and said, 'Jay won't even squash flies in Toad. He just opens the window and shoos them out.'

I tried to laugh, but all the laughter has gone out of my life. I wonder if Tina feels anything at all like I do on the inside . . . bleeding hamburger, crushed bone. I wonder what's keeping me upright. What's keeping her together.

October 7

I made Tina cut school with me and spend the day in Aspen Falls. We had to talk! At first she held back because school is really important to her, but it's important to me too. More important actually, because it's me, the guy, that is eventually going to have to make the living with his brain. Anyway I practically had to kidnap her.

As we were sneaking out the gym door she stopped at the machine and picked up a couple of sandwiches and drinks and Twinkies. Isn't that just like a female, my life is cracking up completely and she stops to get something as mundane as Twinkies.

I hadn't really talked to Tina since . . . well before, except passing 'hi's' almost like we were strangers in the halls, and the night after when she came to work and just whispered, 'I love you, I really do love you through all the eons of time.' I'll never forget those words. They are like red neon in my brain, because I couldn't imagine anything but disgust and loathing in her for me.

All the way up to Aspen Falls and even for a little while when we got there I was uncomfortable. I couldn't say what I really wanted to. It was like we were talking about school things and our families and stuff because we were afraid to get down to the nitty-gritty that really had to be talked about. It was like she was trying to pretend *it* had never happened—maybe that's the way it should be. Anyway, she looked so fragile and helplessly childlike sitting there on the bed of bright-colored leaves that I didn't want to remind her again of nightmares and stuff. I wanted to protect her and love her, adore her. I gathered her into my arms and was gentle with her, for once, more aware and concerned about her needs than mine.

'Can you imagine a more beautiful or wonderful marriage bed?' she whispered afterwards.

I held her close. I never ever ever wanted to let her go! It was the two of us against the world. It always would be.

I had thought on the way up that we would have to break up, that we were not good for each other, that we were feeding each other's weaknesses and fears. But we aren't. Together we're like a full symphony orchestra, not just a flash-in-the-night rock group or a loud dissonant combo but . . . well, like the Mormon Tabernacle Choir singing the 'Hallelujah Chorus.'

I knew, even at the time I thought that, that I should feel blasphemous about connecting those thoughts, but I didn't, I don't now! I want to marry the girl . . . marry her for all time and for all eternity. I know now what that means, what that desire is. NOT just a one night stand . . . not just a relationship . . . but marriage, serious, eternal marriage with children and gobs of relatives and us together, mostly just us together through the rest of high school and college and . . . forever . . . Oh the joy of that thought, the wonder, the sweetness, it wipes out everything that has gone before. Of course, it may take a year or so, but we can wait, anything as good and wonderful as what we've got can do what has to be done! I wonder what's the first step I should take? Should I talk to my father, see my Bishop? Oh Judas, life is so complicated, but so wonderful! So glorious and wonderful and forever! I'm glad I believe in eternity.

> This life is not near enough time
> To love you, Tina.

October 8

Today we went to the football game at Sulphur Spring. We got the crap beat out of us but I really didn't care. Somebody put something in my coke, and I was just grooving along there feeling no pain at all. Screaming and yelling and wishing the hell I could get Tina out of there so I could go after her . . . me and my big plans of being on probation till I was worthy. Judas, what a weak lily-livered bastard I am.

Anyway, after the game we went to Janie's to have pizza. Her parents weren't home so after we'd eaten, someone brought out an Ouija board, then the crystal ball, then the tarot cards, then into Cosmic Alertness . . . imagine, Nancy Nice Janie Jarvis into O too!

It was a fun, nondestructive evening and I've decided that as long as we're just with kids who are into O we're all right. It's the adults that are the freak-outs. I never did hear anything or read anything about the Scott house that I turned in anonymously. I wonder if anything ever happened or if the local narcs just thought it was another crank letter. Oh Judas, I can just see this square old dumb policeman coming up to this nice little supermarket-type lady's door and asking her if she was a witch, if she 'dispensed controlled substances?'

Man, it's *so* underground!!!!!

October 9

I've got to make myself study for a debate Monday and a biology test. I've got to get myself back on the track. I've got to get myself up off my ass . . . auwa . . . think . . . concentrate . . . auwa . . .

Tina called, said not to worry, she loved me. That made me feel better.

October 11

Home for lunch.

I won the debate thumbs up. It was like my mind had computerized every fact I'd ever put there and I could bring them out at will. Man, it's an exhilarating feeling to have that much control over your mental abilities. I received almost a perfect score from the judges, and I was flying, flying, flying until I went to the boys' room and found that, sometime before the debate, Tina had slipped a tiny miniature feathered wanga into my pocket. I was so mad I wanted to flush her down the toilet and it too, but I didn't dare . . . voodoo is supposed to be as powerful for bad as it is for good . . . Oh Judas, I don't believe all that crap! I threw the dumb wanga away and now I'm *really afraid!* Fear is a terrible handicap!

3:45 P.M.

I had my biology test in the afternoon and was so screwed-up I had to get an uppie from Tina to get my head and ass off the floor . . . think I blew it.

October 20

Tina won runner-up in the Miss Apple Hill High contest. She was a little miffed because she wasn't made queen and said it was because I'd been so busy with my own shit that I hadn't used any power in her behalf which really isn't true . . . but then it is. Oh Judas. It's like I'm a puppet. Like I'm controlled and I don't want to be controlled! I want to be me! Free, with *my* free agency to do right or wrong, good or bad, smart or dumb, but still my decisions! I'm not going to let some dumb wanga or anything else control me! Tina said the Ouija board and the crystal ball both had said she would be queen and that only my negativeness made her slip down to princess. Could that be true? Could that possibly be true? Oh crap, this is like living in a primeval culture during the dark ages.

Scary . . . Hairy . . . Scary . . . I just got home from the library and now I wish I hadn't gone. Man, why, why, why did I ever go? Everything I read just makes my position worse.

Al Rossiter Jr., a UPI Science editor from Washington, wrote about a 33-year-old man from Arkansas who became paranoid and then after two weeks in the hospital suffered a fatal heart seizure. An autopsy found no reason for his death but his wife said he had angered a two-headed, who had caused it.

Kenneth Golden, an instructor in the University of Arkansas Psychology Department knew about the two-headed. It's an old woman witch who heals people, and casts spells, both good and bad.

Professor Golden described things in the *American Journal of Psychiatry*. He explained that two-headeds, along with 'conjure doctors,' 'root doctors,' and 'hoodoo men' are believed to be able to trick or hex a person, causing sickness, insanity and death.

Golden says 'Hexing practices are no longer a phenomenon only of rural isolated communities in the deep south. Physicians have provided evidence that voodoo and hexing practices exist as far north as Connecticut.'

Man, if he only knew about the underground kid movements in nice little Apple Hill and Salt Lake and Denver and Las Vegas and all of California, etc. I've met kids from all over and they say it's big and ever growing everywhere. Actually the occult movement is kind of a Pied Piper sort of thing: we want to go but we don't want to go . . . in the end we have no choice . . . we've just got to see what's in that mountain. And besides, the Pied Piper seems so nice at first, so friendly, caring, supportive, sharing and giving only good things, elevating things, all the things kids want and need and don't get enough of at home and school. It's kind of an 'in,' a 'belonging' thing too. We want to belong! We want to be 'in.' The underground secretive part of it just makes the whole setup more compelling and irresistible.

Professor Golden says people in the United States are afraid to tell anyone about hexing practices for fear of being belittled or misunderstood. *He is so right!*

In a way I'm glad I did today's research because now at least I've got someone to present my material to when I get it all gathered, someone that at least has a little background. Maybe Professor Golden will appreciate my findings. Actually I'm sure he will, because there is no way in God's green earth that anyone would get this material unless they'd been there. Man, the vows are so *secretive and so sacred!* I'll only dare break them myself because it's a scientific endeavor and I want to help my fellow man.

October 25

Thirteen of us went up to Mavis Johnson's cabin for the weekend. Tina lied and said she was going with a girl friend, to plan for the Coronation Ball. I lied and said I was going to get away to study for next week's debate in Arizona. Man talk about manipulation, we've got it down to a science.

As I look back I, in a way, feel upped by the weekend—frightened but enlightened—in another way I feel downed, dishonest, disgusted, dishonored. But no matter what I can't deny the *POWERS!* The Satanic Black Powers! I've heard about the devil all my life, that he tempted Adam and Eve, that he misled Cain, that he's always been around to tempt us and get us to do evil, but it's mostly seemed like a fairy story . . . along with elves, or munchkins or Santa Claus. Not now! . . . now I KNOW *HE'S REAL!* That he does exist, that he does, or maybe just on occasion *can*, control parts of this universe!

Long before we started using potions, when my mind was as untouched as it is at this very moment, I saw, through our minds working together, how little piles of twigs can be made to burst into fire by themselves, how a string of beads can be broken without a touch. The string my mom brought me from Hawaii, that had been strung by her missionary cousin. They were special to me and as they rolled into all the corners I started crying, I wasn't stoned or drunk or anything but I started crying. Tina reached up and patted my cheeks and brought me into her arms like a baby. She kissed me gently. Within minutes I realized that she had been chewing, not gum, but a leaf of some kind . . . I was tripping. All the weekend seems vague yet real . . . much of the time I was flying, limitless. I knew all the world, all history. Everything was under me, mine to control. Then the dark side of my soul came forth and rats crawled across me and every kind of vermin and rodent. Tina, who always seemed in command brought me another vial and knowledge began flowing into me again, beyond the darkness of my fears. Again I comprehend all things . . . they're like the lost chord in my memory now. I know they're there, the things of ages past, the things of the ancients, the things of Atlantis. I want them back! Tina said I will have to go into that land beyond this one again to get them, perhaps many times before I can sort the truth from the error, the good from the bad. Am I going to *have* to do that before I can make my great contribution? Oh this ringing in my head still, the pain in the back of my neck . . . the birds. Were they real? Angry? Dangerous? Fear paralyzes clarity, I must gain more control of my thinking so that I can sort the reality from the unreality. For now I am caught between worlds, will I ever get back? Can I bring the hidden sacred treasure of knowledge back with me? Not the knowledge that Satan is their God. That I know! Tina left a note in my pocket when she passed me at the market. I wonder who *she* accepts as her God?

October 27

Tina has convinced me that we've got to stay out of black witchcraft and that the only way to stay in white is for her to start a new coven. I don't know. She says

I'm her master, that she is my slave, and yet I feel like *her* slave. Is she manipulating me?

1:10 A.M.

I've rationally, and after much consideration, decided to get out.

9 P.M.

Saw Tina at the drug store after work. I bought her a coke and told her no matter what, I was through. I pleaded with her to get out too but the look on her face was like all the storms in all the skies that have ever been in the universe. She spat a curse on me and left.

11:30 P.M.

I heard a soft tapping on my bedroom window and opened it as fast as I could. There was a little package but Tina had gone. I ran out the front door, she had disappeared into the shadows. Before I could get down the driveway I heard her father's car screech around the corner. She has returned my wanga in shreds.

I am so low! Oh Tina I know your powers have helped me in my time of need at school, at home, at basketball and soccer. Oh Tina . . . Tina . . . Tina . . . what have you done? You said you would leave me if you had to choose. Why? Why? Why? Why?

I am not your true love. O is!

I sit here, with all the knowledge of the world here at
  my feet.
But the beads are broken and the cross is lost
I can be anything, have anything but the beads are broken . . .

I'm lost alone, everything bad returns and my life is as
  the dust
blown and scattered with the wind gone
I am not . . .
If I haven't the courage to end my life and be finished,
  let it end here . . .
I am not . . .

Tina, I love you. You have saved me many times but
I am lost for sure now. Even your love couldn't keep
me afloat, never think it is your fault, because it isn't.
Return to your 'true love,' O. I am lost . . . and have
nothing but sadness to keep me; let it be known that
all my worldly possessions are yours if you will have
them, if they will remind you of the good times.

Why does this shit sound so melodramatic—even in
death.

October 30

I cannot believe that *everything* can go wrong but it
has! I ran over Kendall's bike which he has left in the
driveway nine million times before and I have never
run over, I lashed out at Chad with a book in my hand
and chipped his front tooth, I fought with mom and
called her a 'bitch' to her face which should get me
something special from dad when he gets home. I absolutely wiped out on my English and my biology
classes, both of which should have been a cinch . . .
and worst of all I wrecked Toad again. Rather, the milk
truck *ran into me* although the asshole denies it.

I feel like Job in the Bible, I literally and truly don't
know how much more I can stand.

I'm pleading sick tonight because there is no way I

can win the debate at the Kiwanis Club. I need that scholarship they're giving, too, and ordinarily it would have been a cinch. I've done my homework, I love the positive side of the subject which I was given 'What's right with America' and—oh hell, it's so primitive and back-woodsey to believe in curses and hexes and shit like that. A lot of this garbage I'm just bringing on myself I know because I'm depressed and filled with guilt feelings. That's what is making me uncoordinated and accident prone and a general emotional misfit. My physical problems are psychosomatic and . . . Oh shit, I've never had saber-toothed crotch crickets before . . . is that all psychosomatic too?

November 6

What a fucked-up world. Bought a few reds and a lid to just keep me together and got *busted!* Not just for using but for pushing. Derrick was in the car when we smelled burned bacon and the dirty asshole shoved his supply under *my* seat. When the pigs frisked us he was clean and it was me that got hit! Life isn't worth poop-de-do.

November 8

I am under house arrest. I feel like I am five years old. Mama, may I go to the potty? Number one? Number two? Screw you! Well at least I'm going to have lots of time to think and to get my mental processes straight. I only get to go to school and work. No TV, no record player, no radio, no phone, no friends. What are they trying to do to me? Solitary confinement drives even hardened criminals loony, or maybe gets them straightened out. Maybe I needed this! Maybe it's just what I needed. At least I'm going to work in that direction. Take a detached look at myself, my general characteristics, my goals and interests. Besides, the old lady demands that I do it! With or without her insistence I had to make some changes in my life, though.

I must *want* to change now
I was placed in this room to provide a motivation for change, i.e., I wouldn't be let out until I realized and accomplished certain things.

Am I happy as I am now?
Am I headed in the direction of accomplishing worthwhile goals in life?
Am I living up to the trust and love that has been invested in me by people who care?
Will I be happy in one year from now by staying the way I am?
No one else will change for me, I must change myself.
Why should I change? Why should I want to change?

1. To get out of this room (immediate, temporary, not important as such).
2. So I can get along with Mom and Dad.
3. So I can accomplish more with my time.
4. So I can develop true skills and talents.
5. So I can set myself in the right direction for accomplishing the things I want to.

My Biggest Mistakes—
Not wanting to help (change) myself, deceiving

myself into thinking I am happy as I am or that
change would come about without really trying to
change, or wanting to change.
Procrastinating about changing.

I do want to change.

In order to overcome faults, something must be
done.
In order to overcome

1. Conceit—become less selfish, see other person's view of myself. Put my point of view
   outside of self.
2. Disrespectfulness—acknowledge love and
   trust of others.
3. Lying—remember beauty in truth.
4. Momentary pleasure—before doing anything
   stop and think if it will affect long-range goals
   the right way.
5. Too much individualism—go out of way to get
   along with others, don't think in terms of just
   self.
6. Procrastination—start immediately on tasks,
   do hardest things first.
7. Laziness—motivate myself to hard work, as-
   sociated with long-range goals. Anything constructive accomplished is beautiful.
8. Closedmindedness—listen to others, see others' point of view.
9. Hypocrisy—commit self to ideals and standards, truly live them.
10. Non-congeniality—put self out to get along,
    acknowledge that it's the only way to world
    peace. Understand others.

11. Wastefulness—acknowledge work required for things.
12. Insincerity—Always express true feelings unless they are malicious. Overcome malicious feelings.
13. Hot temper—Control temper. Do unto others . . .
14. Being sorry when should have acted—Don't be hypocritical, if something is wrong, correct it.
15. Unorganized—Acknowledge importance of organization.
16. Self-centeredness—Let world revolve around others.
17. Rebelliousness—Accept social ideas as important, think before blindly rebelling.
18. Apathy—Get involved as much as possible.

Basic Faults—

Laziness—Recognize importance and beauty of constructive work.

Selfishness—Place point of view outside self.

Check long-range goals, get involved with others.

November 9

It's like I'm no longer a member of the human race. I can't relate. I had lunch with Brad and Dell and we couldn't communicate. They're on a different, lighter wavelength, talking about basketball and girls and unimportant concepts. They don't know how it is with me, trying to get my deep, seriously deep concepts back into a working order, an existing order. It's so easy and kind of floating on the surface for them. I hope they

never have to go through the kind of soul searching that
I am going through.

I'm working harder than I've ever worked in my life,
but I'm not making it in class. I'm just not with it, out
of sync—what's wrong?

I've got to pretend I don't care, that I'm not really
trying my hardest, not really working my ass off. Lie
to my family . . . lie to my teachers . . . lie to my
friends . . . lie to Tina . . .

Oh help, I'm drownding!

       d-
          r-
              o-w-n-d-
                    i-
                         n-
                            g!
                                glub. . . .

Tina . . . (my mind is so fucked-up I can't even think
of the word that means tries to stay away from me) . . .
oh yeah . . . ignores me.

'Got my shit together'
Definition: I've learned how to play it cool, I've
got some ideas worked out.

SOMEBODY

I am very, very lonely,
I've got myself and that's all, beside the burden
I'm carrying. The burden of change. The burden
of being myself. (My only possession.) If I lose
myself by conforming to be exactly what 'they'

want me to be I lose the only thing I've got. I need
somebody to tell me some of my ideas are right.
I know hope is bad, no argument, but shit . . .
(What about everything else, O?)
I need somebody to believe in me!
(Somebody to love, baby)

November 11, 8 A.M.

Mom and dad, can't you see what you're doing? You're
driving me back to that which I am trying to get away
from! That which is more dangerous and destructive
than rudeness, lack of respect, carelessness, immoral-
ity, even doping! Please, don't do this to me!!!!

Mom, I know your cousin Cistine is a psychologist,
but don't make her leave her family and come baby-sit
me as my warden. I can't stand that much pressure,
honestly I can't. I'll rebel, and go back with *them*, don't
make me do that! It's hard enough as it is to resist
crawling back to Tina, begging, pleading, offering,
selling out my soul to her.

At night I can smell their incense, taste their vials
. . . on a gut level—I can't resist.

I've tried to pray but it's like a black cocoon has been
thrown down over me and I can't get through. Oh
please, please, please, rest . . . please sleep, come to
me . . . be my companion, my refuge, my ally.

Aunt Cistine was just *allowed*, by the permission and
almighty power of my parents, to come into my room.
Aunt Sis, the family shrink, will take all my secret acts,
too dreadful for the local headlines. She will carefully
sweep them into the closet—that is, after she's discussed them with every member of the clan over their
fancy, gluttonous dinners. I've heard the relatives talk

about little cousin Cally getting pregnant and having to get married . . . oh how they smacked their mouths over that one . . . barely fourteen years old . . . from *our family, our bloodlines, our genealogy!!!* And Uncle Martin . . . when they found he was foolin' around . . . I think it was the reason they called the special party, not great-grandpa Talley's eightieth birthday at all—cancer, deaths, handicapped babies . . . everything, a special occasion to hash and rehash family secrets. Well, if they think I'm going to tell anybody, especially Sis, anything, they're wasting their curiosity. I wouldn't tell that screwed-up bitch the time of day.

8:30 P.M.
When Old Sis started really pressuring me about how much she cared, I told her to try sticking all those emotions where the sun never shines.

She still wouldn't give up, and finally she got me so fragmented I told her what a degenerate old whore I really thought she was, trying to get her kicks out of hearing about my transgressions. I wonder what she worms out of the kids at school she works with? Is that how the old bitch turns on? Do she and Charlie discuss those things in the middle of the night and then, fired up as hell, pretending . . . substituting . . . reach out and grab at each other?

Oh shit, I'm the one that's fucked-up degenerate, crazy! Not Sis, not Charlie, not my folks, not anybody else in the whole world.

> My sins press
> Down upon my breast
> I cannot rest.
> They crush me

And I cannot sleep
I pray the Lord my soul to keep.

November 11

Today after school I really tried to talk to Sis. It was
nice to have someone—anyone—to verbalize with. My
sprained ankle keeps me out of sports and my fucked-
up mind keeps me antisocial in class. And Tina . . .
Judas, I love that woman so much. She stopped me in
the hall and looked at me with those deep purple eyes.
They were very purple today because she was wearing
a kitten soft purple sweater and tight white pants. I
could smell her . . . feel her more than physical wonders. She rubbed against me and whispered, 'Oh Jay, I
love you *so much*. Why have you cut me out? Why
won't you let me help you?' A little sob tumbled out
of her throat, 'Please let me help you, Jay . . . I *love*
you!'

All the masculine instincts in the world surged over
me, a beaten person become alive. Tina wasn't trying
to hurt, hadn't cut me out. I'd cut her out, and Brad
and Dell and everyone else too—being paranoid and
self-demeaning and antisocial only got me down—not
them!

Sis came in after dinner and I let it all hang out, at
least everything but . . . well, the parts I don't even
like to think about . . . that I'm pretending didn't really
happen. Actually I guess that's about half, or maybe
even two-thirds of what's happened in the last couple
of years.

Then she started pushing too hard again and said I
wasn't trying . . . I don't know what kicked me off, but
I told her to pull down her pants and try sticking her

own head up her ass, that it's a pretty hard and painful position.

She stormed out and I'm glad. I hope I never see her again, or anyone else for that matter. This room is like a tomb anyway. I might as well just lie down . . . give up . . . and take my last breath. I wish it was that easy and I would.

At least I know Sis is professional. She won't go blabbing. She's got some shit in her own life she'd like to keep buried, she said. I wonder if I really can trust her? I've got to trust someone, got to unload before I explode! Would she prove out to be Benedict Arnold II? No, she wouldn't . . . she wouldn't! Tomorrow I'm going to trust her, lay the whole load on her, get it out of my craw and on her shoulders. Judas, what a relief that is going to be. Once I heard President Oaks say that when we read and see and do bad things *they stay with us,* when we eat bad things we *regurgitate* them. He reasoned that it was a shame the mind, in that respect, wasn't as reasonable as the stomach. Well, my mind is going to be! I'm going to puke up everything, but everything in good old Sissy's lap, and then forget the hell about it forever!

10 P.M.
Dad just came in mad as a hornet. It seems that my good old Aunt Sissy, that I was just learning to trust and honor, has betrayed me. Apparently she discussed everything I'd said with my family and the police. I can hardly think, I hurt so much. Nobody will ever know how deeply disillusioned and hurt I am.

And I'm mad! MAD! . . . MAD! . . . MAD! . . . MAD!!!!

BENEDICT ARNOLD II

So man, what do ya do when your family (and or however the hell you spell) has been cheating you, selling you out, screwing you over? She doesn't give shit for me that's for sure. If she did she would try and understand the hassles you have and the silent apologies but she is so blinded by the fact she thinks she's been through the world and knows the shit. She doesn't know her head from her ass (at least that's the impression I get after today and all of the other stuff I've found out just lately). She may have been through the mill and had a lot of experience and all that but it didn't do her any good and it's not going to do me any good if she doesn't know how to run herself. I really thought she was cool and had my interest in mind. What a bunch of B.S. She hates my guts but I'm not going to get hassled by it 'cause that's what she wants. She's waiting for me to slip up so she can screw me. The only hassle for her is I'm not going to screw up. So Sis—you live your life and let me work out my problems my way. You may hold all the cards now so I'll just have to play your little game for a while. But after that, bug off.

Yeah, after writing that little bit I feel a heck of a lot better. That's what this book is for I guess. To get the hassles out of my system. I don't know how much of that stuff I just wrote is really true but she does seem to have turned against me. Her shit just doesn't fit my head. I wish they could understand. It would be so cool if we could get along (me and the family) but they just don't understand. (I guess I kinda blew it so that they are sure they're right now.) At any rate, I do feel less hostile and I suppose that's constructive.

November 12

I couldn't stand the pressure at school this afternoon so I thumbed home, bent on hot-wiring Toad and just taking off for California or Mexico or somewhere. Cutting-out seemed like the only thing to do.

When I got here it was obvious that dad had read my thoughts because he had put Toad in the garage with a new big lock that I couldn't get the hell open. I knew mom was at Relief Society so I even tried to break the damn thing with a crowbar but I couldn't. Failure seems to have become a critical part of my life, maybe even a fatal malady for me.

Just as I was about to bash my head against the wall I noticed the pickup in front of the boat, anybody could hot-wire that! After I'd got it out I tried to get the motorcycle in the bed. I'd take them up the canyon and maybe dirt racing would get me put together enough so I could hang on. At this point I knew running away wasn't the answer, some dangerous racing and a few physical hurts to concentrate on might be, I reasoned.

Well, the bike was so damned heavy there was no way I could get both wheels up at one time, even far enough over so I could push them in. So, after I'd smashed all my toes and broken two fingernails down to the quick and hurt my ankle again, I decided to build a ramp and drive the sucker up on the bed. It seemed like a neat idea until I tried it—once, twice, maybe three or four times. Finally I decided I'd have to go way to the end of the driveway, eighty or ninety feet, and really start the old machine gunning before I could get enough power to take it up the ramp, especially since the driveway was a little slippery.

Success? *WRONG!* I not only went into the truck bed—but into the back of the cab! Wrenching the front wheel on the bike and cracking the window and making a big old hairy dent in the cab, besides throwing me head first end-over-end over the top, down the windshield and onto the hood.

Well, at least I've got something to concentrate on besides my old problems now, like: breaking the rules for house arrest, wrecking the bike, wrecking the truck, a possible broken nose and a couple of loose front teeth, scratches, bruises and lacerations. But hell, I don't care! It was exciting! The most exciting thing that's happened in my life in what seems like eons.

Even the blood tasted good in my mouth and the loose teeth will give me an excuse to go to the dentist for nitrous.

When mom got home I was stretched out on my bed. I had decided to manipulate and pretend I was really hurt, that would greaten their concern for me and lessen their anxiety about the dirt bike and the truck. . . . It worked! Man, did it work!

I even pretended I was a little incoherent when mom came in and I had let the blood from my nose and mouth drip and dry on my face and shirt and bed. She was ready to call an ambulance but I convinced her I could make it to the car with her help. It was like being in the theater. Me leaning on her and giving an occasional groan.

I was embarrassed in the emergency room of the hospital because mom had called before we left home and there were nurses and two doctors waiting. Of course that was just because mom and dad knew everybody in town I'm sure, or maybe they were just curious to see what the Bozo had done to himself this time. Anyway, now I'm all tucked into my own clean little bed and everyone is so concerned about my physical well-being the whole other pile of shit has been forgotten.

November 13

Man, I look awful, two black eyes, a kind of tin grin retainer on my teeth till they're tight again, all the skin peeled off one cheek, the other one black and purple and blue. I look like a clown but, man, am I ever getting attention. It's like the olden days! Me, the man on the flying dirt bike. It should be embarrassing but it isn't. It's funny and fun, fun, fun, happy funny fun! I guess ripping off the establishment is the best part. They're treating me like I'm the most precious thing in the world. Motorcycles and trucks can be replaced . . . but me! . . . *WOWIE!* I'm back where I belong.

Tina came by this afternoon. By my house! Into my room! The doc had said I was to rest as much as possible for a few days. So I was just stretched out on my bed getting into my new tape when I heard this voice . . . her voice. It was like a dream and I didn't want to wake up. She'd gone home from school and made me chocolate chip cookies . . . isn't that bitchin'? Tina the little homemaker, the chocolate chip baker . . . Oh the joy.

She stayed for two hours and we just talked . . . saying nothing in words . . . everything in thoughts . . .

Man, I'm so spaced out by the very thought and nearness of her. Tina and Jay . . . TINA AND JAY!

I've been so alone and lonely and unbelonging for so long . . .

November 14
First day for 'T'.

Well today I gave my first news report for KOVO, kinda weird. 'Big Sister's' still here and still there's the plastic 'play the game' front between me and her, and underneath the hate and disgust. But of more importance, Tina and I finally came to grips about our relationship. I love her and she loves me. That's all there is to it except that our minds are still growing and this may cause a hassle, but what will be will be.

A happiness, a hopelessness, two children on the
    wing
A loving look, a story book and sacred hymns to
    sing.

I have invested my heart. There is a chance that it will be broken but also a chance at unlimited happiness.

The time . . .
So—
ANOTHER
(better?)
DAY
(a thousand hearts, two thousand eyes, a million tears)
away—

November 16
Isn't it funny that down times are SO DOWN and up times are SO UP!

My relationship with Tina has never been better. My relationships at school, at home . . . I appreciate everything, everybody! They appreciate me. Mom apologized about Cistina. She knew even at the time she called her that it wasn't right to get a family member involved in something that they should be detached about. But people do weird things when they're under pressure. Nobody knows that better than I do.

Tina has gotten out of the supernatural kick just like I wanted her to . . . except for Derrick. She went through the bit to make him admit that he was the holder, not me. I'm trying not to think about that scene but it is strange that Derrick admitted to his parole officer that it was his shit. Why in the world would he ever have admitted that except . . . Oh Judas, I'm not going to let myself think about it, the whole thing is a bummer.

Chaddy brought me home a little handprint he'd made in clay, in primary. He made it especially for me. For my desk. What a precious, sweet, little guy. I've got to be a good example to him!

Today I heard about a high school forensic meet in California. I do hope I'm picked to represent our school, our state.

All my teachers are so neat they're letting me do outside work for extra credit so I can pick up what I've flushed the last couple of weeks . . . or past forever . . . it seems like forever, since I've been in the harmonious swing of things.

November 17

I'm free. Derrick having admitted it was his shit threw the whole case. Everyone thinks he was just in my car. That I was just giving him a ride. He didn't mention I had bought from him and I didn't mention it either. *Man, that is strange!* Nobody in their right mind would have—just up and out of nowhere have something that heavy laid on them when they didn't have to. Forget it, man . . . forget it! You can't even understand the powers that cause television, electricity or the telephone to work. How can you expect with your little finite mind— lay off it, baby! It's too heavy. Think of good things, like tonight . . . the game . . . Toad . . . Tina . . . love, wonder, belonging, real belonging. Oh I'm so hungry for her, so hungry and thirsty and starved and I saw her just this afternoon . . . but I can't see her enough, be with her enough. I wish we could get married! Did I write that? Yes I did and it's true! Man, is it ever true! I want her for twenty-four hours of every day like I've never wanted anything in my life before.

1:30 P.M.

The game is over, the dance is over, goodies at the Blue Moo are over, but my life has just begun! Tina and my life has just begun! She is home in her little bed, with her covers pulled up over her little head like a child. But she is going to be my wife. She said 'Yes.' It is up to me to make preparations for our future, for my taking care of her. How? I must figure out how! I don't want to wait until I'm in college. She doesn't either. In primitive societies people just get married when they are ready; but in our ultra super-sophisticated one, first we must have the education, then we must have the money, then we must have the material necessities. Shit—none of those things are important, only *love is!* And I love her! She loves me! We cannot exist without each other. That is all that is important! Our happiness, our immediate and complete rapture and happiness. I'll find a way! Together, we'll find a way.

November 18

Man, I went against a jock from Arizona High who's got a brain like a sword. He's so sharp he about slaughtered me. If I do as poorly tomorrow as I did today I'm out! I know it! I can feel it. He really knocked me on my ass. Tomorrow he'll just shove it up to my eye balls.

Tina called, she begged me to let her use voodoo but I can't. Man, I want to go to the Nationals *so bad!* I'm tempted to try anything I can, even *that!* After all, what can it hurt? If it's so much hokey-pokey I'll just skin my ass some more. If it works? I don't want to admit it but *I know* it works! It's like faith in reverse. With faith you have to use strength to make things happen. With—whatever it is—you have to just fight yourself and your normal inclinations and cultural patterning and brainwashing and programming so that you can let your cosmic consciousness do its powerful thing.

1:43 A.M.

I met with Tina and eleven other kids at eleven-thirty. For about an hour we talked about Cosmic Consciousness. We thirteen and the universe were one. There was no division of supernatural and natural. Together we placed ourselves in harmony with the harmony that governs all the planets in space as well as the tiny atom. The consciousness that directs and controls the physical universe pulsated in every cell of our beings. We were linked with infinity and could draw upon its power at will.

Together we shredded a wanga in my opponent, Jack Fry's name, then we all concentrated in absolute togetherness: bad vibes, physical and mental disharmony, physical sickness, mental discord. A curse, a hex, a tonoa.

November 19

I can't believe it! I massacred Jack. The word was around even before the debate started that he had come down with a terrible cold during the night and had wanted to withdraw but his coach wouldn't let him. It wouldn't have mattered though if he hadn't been, well, unfortunate (was it a coincidence?) because I was in fine form, on top of things. It was a neat feeling to verbally disarm and defeat a foe. I wonder if this is how a hit man feels in the Mafia when he's done his job well. Oh crap, the two things don't have anything to do with each other. I'm just mixing Gadianton robbers with reality. I've decided one thing—I'm *not* going to try to figure things out anymore! I'm just going to accept a new power like my grandparents must have accepted radio and my parents must have accepted TV

Tina and I are closer than we've ever been. I think the short time apart made us even more desirous of looking only for the good in each other, working only towards our future. Made her more interested in my happiness and well-being than in her own, and made me the same about her. It's a wonderful relationship. I support her one hundred percent as school princess and vice-president. She, in turn, is my staunchest ally in all endeavors. I feel so happy I want to go out and do something exciting, but what? Run down to the market and squeeze the Charmin?

November 21

Tina's got me uptight again. She's pushing the coven bit! She promises she'll use only white witchcraft! I feel skittish about the whole thing. Astra, the Rosicrucian setup, Cosmic Consciousness, and even some kinds of voodoo like Wanga I can understand and go along with, after all they're quite literally mind over matter . . . An extension of Christianity, I can handle that and things from the ancients—ancient secrets, ancient combinations, powers that have been lost to mankind—but witchcraft? Uh-uh, I don't think so.

Tina came and tapped on my window at midnight. I crawled out and we went and sat in her dad's car and talked till almost daylight. I guess she's got me partly, well mostly, convinced that actually her coven would be more like a clique trying to scientifically understand and learn to use powers that have long been lost to mankind, than just some kind of cult worshipping nutso group.

If we're going to use these unknown powers just for good like we talked about (no more cutting down, even like we did on Jack Fry at the debate), if we're just going to use it to make the most of ourselves, improve and expand our own potentials and powers and outputs and help others . . . well, it's kind of exciting and exhilarating when I think about it in that context, even Dell and Brad would go for that.

November 24

I guess everyone is seeking answers, particularly about the super-natural, about our psychic selves, especially me and Tina and Dell and Brad.

I don't know where Tina got so much literature but it's like a crash course we're taking. This search into the slumbering cosmic power that all humans possess, but few understand and use, is becoming the central theme of our lives. Cosmic Seeking does not deprive us of anything good though indeed it feeds those attributes and beliefs: our relation to God, intuition, meditation, auras, ESP, life after death, the oversoul and multitudes of other mystical spiritual studies.

Every day at noon we thirteen will meet, maybe in groups of three or four and relive the secret of initiation, erase a little karma so we can be more liberated. Sometimes the stuff seems quite childish, other times it blows me away. Like today, we were sitting in the last booth at the Blue Moo, and nobody else was around. Tina pulled both the knife and the fork across the table by mental magnetism, then knocked six cups, over by the kitchen, off the shelf, onto the floor, one by one. She's positively fantastic, and doesn't seem to have to concentrate very hard at all anymore. I can sometimes do it but it drains me completely, in fact doesn't seem worth the price. Tina keeps assuring me it will come, in time, which is probably right, because all things that one persists in doing become easier, not that the thing changes, but that the person's ability to do increases.

Sometimes, just to test our powers, we choose a person and for instance concentrate on his neck; within seconds he's scratching like something bit him or something. It's an amazing force! We must always remember that and be very careful to use it in the right way. That is the important thing! Tina says that's the trouble with black witchcraft, they are prostituting a wondrous jurisdiction. I'm going to use all the power I can get to reach the goals I've set for next year.

I must not give myself too much, yet enough to keep me stimulated, alert, and ever with an open and curious mind! It has become my conclusion that as people grow older they close themselves into their own little worlds, indeed *lock themselves* in! Shut the windows of their eyes, bolt the exit and entry of their ears. They are not looking for new ideas, concepts, powers, indeed they will not accept them if they are presented. Not so with me! Forever I will be looking towards the infinite, the unknown, the evolving, the omnipresent, the omnipotent. My mind and my being will be open. I will search . . . and search . . . and search!

One time when I was young and we were out camping, Dad stumbled across a new cave. With a rope he scrambled down into the hole, literally just a gash in the ground, then asked me and my cousins to jump down to him in the darkness. None of them dared to but me. Sure I was afraid, afraid as hell, yet curious beyond my ability to bear. Besides, I trusted dad. I knew he wouldn't let me dash myself against the rugged rocks as I am sure my cousins, standing in the bright rim of sunshine up above, thought he would. No, my father caught me in his arms and together, with his small flashlight, we explored caverns and subterranean grottos, each more beautiful than the one before it. A miniature Carlsbad Caverns, with stalactites and stalagmites, reaching down to the floor and up to the ceiling. The colors were muted and eerie and an occasional bat flopped in the air high above our heads. We passed chasmal, gaping, yawning holes, some with the sounds of water gurgling in their depths.

It was my experience! . . . MINE ALONE . . . because I dared to take it! Dared to tackle the unknown! I dare to do it now! Dare pull my metal pen towards me from its holder without physical help, I cause the candle on my desk to burn higher or lower as my mental strength controls the amount of oxygen it is given, or whatever the explanation to the phenomenon is. A phenomenon only because I do not understand the principle upon which it works. I will not be afraid of things I do not understand!

I think of the caveman, surely he must have considered fire magic, and been afraid, as has mankind with each great step of science taken since that time.

I will not be among the blind! Or those who will not see or hear!

My rituals each night become more amazing! How grateful I am to Tina for bringing me into this new dimension.

> I love her more than life or death
> Or lives beyond this life.
> Existence could not be,
> On any plane,
> Without her smile;
> The tender look upon her face.
> As master-slave we'll bring extension
> To the human race.

Tina has found a spot where we can meet regularly. It's so difficult practicing our arts in areas where unbelievers may interrupt at any time. She says once we can concentrate and use our disciplines completely we will see miraculous growth in our abilities and controls.

November 27

I hate the superstitious namby-pamby of having to have thirteen people, and the candle and crap, but I guess it's like having to add the extra two spoonsful of flour to a cake mix when you live at a high altitude, so it won't fall in the middle. Little seemingly unimportant laws govern big things and their outcome. Anyway, somehow Tina got the key to a little supply shack just next to the cemetery. It doesn't have any windows but it does have a small coal stove so I guess we're set for a place, especially since I'm sure it's rarely used except in the summer, for mowing and weeding and fertilizing supplies. Anyway, the place isn't important, although she acts like it is, it's just having privacy.

We are entering into a strange new world. The people around us are so fascinated with life on other planets and yet they do not even try to know the wonders of the unknown that are right now, right *here* on this one.

Tonight we put Tina in a suspended state. Glen had brought his dad's stethoscope and blood pressure thing and there was no sign of life, no heartbeat, no pulse. When we lifted the lids of her eyes they were as blank as those of a dead cat or any other deceased creature I've ever seen. I'll never let her do that again. In case something goes wrong. We're not into it enough to control the unknown. We can make things happen but we don't know the cause . . . only the effect. It's too dangerous, especially for her.

I'm into cutting myself and being mentally able to slow down or speed up or even stop the bleeding altogether. It's fascinating! What a priceless boon this will be to medicine. No medication, only one's control over their own body! *What miracles have we stumbled across?* They must be used for good when we understand them a little more and can present them intelligently to the outside. These new concepts are *so stimulating! So challenging, so exciting!*

It's strange how the occult works, though. Twice I've tried to present these unknown powers that we are experimenting with to adults in a scientific atmosphere, once to my science teacher Mr. Baugh, and once to my seminary teacher, just to show my control of my own body, but I guess there was so much unbelief and mockery in the atmosphere that I couldn't work against it or I was so nervous and uptight I wasn't functioning properly on my own level. Anyway, it's the shits knowing about all this wonder and miraculous power and not being able to share it with the medical or scientific world. Maybe we just don't know how to present it, more likely it just has to be perfected first. I can just see someone trying to present television fifty years ago, or radio seventy-five years ago. Imagine then, trying to explain how the room is filled with electro-magnetic waves, some of them forming sound and some of them forming pictures when they are drawn together in the right way. Those people, being informed, would be running to call the nut factory to make reservations for new inmates. But I can't blame them. A year ago I would never NEVER NEVER have believed some of the things I'm experiencing now. It's scary but it shouldn't be, no more scary than electricity, or the telephone, or TV or radio, or even how the garage door works from a button. Those things are all kind of magic too, it's just that no one wants to use that word for things they can't comprehend or explain.

I just found out there is a Dr. Hans Enger at UCLA who's becoming accepted and respected in working with phenomena. He's only one of many around the country. He says he has successfully used 'energy healing' on scores of patients, even though he admits he has no idea why the procedures work.

In one spectacular demonstration he showed his technique by relieving the throbbing pains of a lady who suffered an agonizing nerve disorder of the neck and face and head.

This lady, a desperate Jane Elliot of Wood River, Ill., said, 'He stood over me and put his hand above my head. Immediately I felt this tremendous charge of electricity pass through me, like the light bulb into the socket. Then the pain seemed to scatter.'

For ten days Dr. Enger treated her, then she was 'entirely free of pain.'

Oh, the wonder of it! Why isn't everybody in the world as curious and as searching as are we?

> Oh Tina
> I love thee
> And the sacred ancient truths
> You've brought to me.

November 28

Today I gave my handmade announcement of our wedding to twenty-six friends. It's going to be a full moon and a clear night (the weatherman says and he's GOT to be right this time for a change). After the debate in the auditorium and the dinner at the Country Club, and the Sweater Fling in the gym, wow! I'm not sure I can stand the wonder of it! Our marriage! Tina has planned all the particulars. She and Meg and Rosalee have been like three sparrows chirping, flying and roosting up and down the halls. Everyone thinks the excitement is about the dance, because all three of them are in student government or some kind of control at school, but anyway, the excitement is about us! Not me and her—myself and her, or however the hell it goes grammatically—in reality we'll be no more *two* but *one!* Oh man, I'm not sure I can stand this much joy. I could kiss a cactus!

November 30

When I found out Tina was having our wedding in the cemetery, by the big tomb, I about died. It was like making a mockery of the whole thing. I knew we'd invited only the kids connected with O and it was to be part of the sacred ancient sacrament but . . . Anyway, it was fantastic! The moon was perfectly round and it wasn't even all that cold. By the single little black candle, which we certainly didn't need for light, we went through the ritual of eternal slavery to each other although I, the male, would always technically be the master. Then we each cut our tongues and let the blood pour into each other's mouths. It was Nirvana. We were one! One blood, one toulca, one being!

Rosalee passed the sacred vial around and we performed the ritual of extending ourselves to extend others. Bright colors and lightning flashes streaked through the sky. Sometimes the colors exploded like rockets on the Fourth of July, both in and out of our heads.

When the chanting started Martin brought in a teensy mewing kitten. With one twist he wrung its little neck. Instantly we all put forth every gram of power at our command to bring it back to life again, that being the supreme taloa.

I don't know how the others felt but I concentrated until I thought my whole being was going to detonate, then I relaxed . . . calling the cat's karma . . . magnetizing its karma . . . but in vain, we had not yet advanced to that plane.

In a way the stilled kitten ruined the evening. We

were progressing—but apparently not far enough to call back the karma of even a kitten that had departed at the same second we strove to bring it back. I ran my hand over its soft little body and felt a tear drip down my face. We had failed! Even during the high time of the consecrated marriage ceremony, we had failed! Someday we would bring spirits into the world through birth, that was an accepted way, but to bring the kitten's spirit back into its own body, before it had hardly had time to leave this sphere of existence had . . . Oh Judas, I'm off into the areas that blow my mind, or is it just that knowing Tina and I are married yet still have to sleep alone in our own beds that is driving me bananas? I'm going crazy. The saber-toothed crotch crickets are leaving their abode, are taking over the whole of my body, inside and out. I am dying, dying for you, Tina! I need you, want you! This is ridiculous, not normal on our wedding night! I can't let myself think about it. Oh sweet sleep, where is thy handmaiden, the sleeping pill?

December 3

I can't believe that Tina and I are married. I see her in the halls and I want to take her right there. I don't care about teachers, friends, classmates, anything. I want her! Want her! Want her! Actually I'm not *that* depraved, but oh Judas, it's bad! Almost worse than before.

Our lives have become one giant INSTEAD OF! Instead of going to assembly we go get it on in Toad. Instead of sports or practice or any extra-curricular activities we're off experimenting, studying, in the occult, sometimes I feel like I'm drowning, being sucked under in some way that I cannot understand, but it's so exciting, so thrilling, so exotically and hypnotically compelling! The mundane is becoming so much more super-mundane . . . school, family, etc. I'm beginning to live for my O experiences. They're more fulfilling than anything—life, death, drugs, even sex! I couldn't possibly tell Tina that, or does she possibly feel the same way? In a way, I'm almost sure she does!

I've begun to study Sanskrit. Swami means 'self mastery in all things,' that is where I want to be.

Tina showed me some material during lunch that is fragmenting. We're getting there. The Menninger Foundation in Topeka, Kansas, is aware of some of the powers. They, under the strict supervision of their Voluntary Controls Program research department had Swami Rama leave his ashram in northern India so they could check his mind-body relationships, checking his mind's ability and capacity to regulate his physiological processes, especially those functions usually labeled involuntary or automatic. During the demonstrations Swami Rama *stopped* his heart for 17 seconds and produced differences of temperature in the palms of his hands at will. The Asians are so advanced. How long will it take us to learn their High Wisdoms in the simple things? Westerners are so enamored by the pursuit and worship of power and riches that they are unaware or unconcerned about the wonder of the unseen and the unexplored mysteries and truths around them.

December 4

It is so advantageous and stimulating being a man, even in our society. Dell and Brad and I are taking off with Mel for Colorado tomorrow afternoon right after school. Our parents are content thinking we are going skiing for the weekend. Life was just so yuck—nothing—dull today till this came up. Poor Tina is sick because she couldn't manipulate her way into the trip. It must be tough beans being a girl.

I'm as excited as a little kid before his birthday! Will the Bootan really work? I've seen voodoo work, not once but enough times to have accepted it on a proven basis. Now . . . WOW . . . a higher power . . . BOOTAN!

This morning was like the morgue, this afternoon is like starting the circus cycle!

Hurry Friday, come on! Hurry, hurry, hurry Friday! I'm giving up a big debate in Washington for this chance . . . Please, please let it be worth it.

Tonight Dell and Mel and Brad and I sat in the back of his dad's van and talked and marveled. Mel's eighteen. He went up to a Bootan ceremony two years ago. He said it was practiced more then than it is now. In fact, he quoted John Welsh, some kind of biggie in the National Cattlemen's Association, who said that in 1975 and 1976 there were about 3,000 cattle mutilations.

I can't allow myself to think of Bootan as that. It's a force as real as faith and stuff that people understand and accept. Mel says most seekers now use small animals for rites but that cattle are still the supreme gifters, like the hallowed bulls in ancient Egypt. I guess the ancient Egyptians knew many of the sacred secrets that have been lost.

Will tomorrow ever come? Ohhh . . . mellow, mellow . . . yellow eyes.

December 7

The whole weekend seems unreal. Driving along pasture roads until Mel found exactly the right bull. Mel's bow with the electric arrow made from a many times increased battery-powered cattle prodder, but with a charge strong enough to stun said bull. Our rushing to the giant beast as he tried to struggle then fell to the ground.

I remember the blood sloshing up into my ears as we raced into the pasture. Dell held the flashlight while Mel made precise little surgical cuts in exactly the right places. He had practiced in the van on a big chart we'd ripped off from the market showing a side of beef. Oh, first we siphoned off the blood from a careful tiny slash in a vein, put it into gobs of gallon jars we'd ripped off from the A&W and the caterers, trying not to spill a drop. It would be used as part of a ritual when we returned home. Mel, like a surgeon, cut out the eyes, tongue and balls. Then we had to go for another animal. Taking all the parts from one would lessen the power they retained. Each organ was immediately sealed in a fruit jar, and whisked off to the van. That kept me and Brad jumping. Besides, the bull smelled like nothing I'd ever smelled before and made strange gurgling sounds in his throat and belly even though he was dead. It was bad enough to see the eyes and balls in jars. I don't know how Dell managed to watch Mel do it. Actually none of it really seemed *real!*

We were half way through before I was even aware that all the cattle that had drifted away from us were mooing and making other strange noises that I didn't know cows made. It was spooky and I wanted to get the hell out of there. When Mel finished and we sprinted across the field with the last of our stuff, I wondered if anyone would ever suspect we had been there. Mel had had his knives so sharp they had gone through the cow's hide almost without effort and each cut had been so clean and almost bloodless that I had been amazed. A few flies on the cuts and no one would ever know what had happened except that parts were missing and that jars and jars of blood had disappeared.

In the van, Mel and I sat in the back while Dell bounced back towards the highway with his lights off, all of us grateful for the big clear moon. Even with its light, however, we hit chuck holes and rocks, without it we might have high centered at any point and found ourselves in a mess I don't know how the hell we would have gotten out of. After we'd been on the highway for about half an hour Mel had Dell pull over and we added anticoagulant something to the blood and parts. It was important, Mel said, to keep them as exact as possible. *I couldn't wait!* Kept wondering if Bootan really would work! The excitement was intoxicating!

After about another hour of driving we took off on a second side road and started looking for a cow that came up to all Mel's requirements. It didn't take long to find one and soon we had downed it and slit its vein also, the tiniest little incision. This time each of us took turns drinking the warm blood directly from the female animal. It was hard to get down because it came out in such great spurts, and was so hot, so much hotter than I had expected, or maybe it was me. Again we drained the blood, this time not so carefully, and took a few parts, Mel having informed us that all living things are composed of both female and male whatevers.

It was a relief when we got back on the highway and started heading towards home. Mel wouldn't even let us stop to piss, though, and the excitement had about exploded our bladders.

All four of us squeezed up in the front area and Mel told us how ranchers from at least twenty-two states had reported cattle mutilations. Man, O must be even bigger than *I* thought! Brad, who was driving, slowed down when Mel added that various rural groups had gone together and put rewards up, some as high as $25,000.

The blood we had drunk was supposed to have given us the strength of the animal and at that time I'm sure if we had stopped we could have lifted the van. We felt like TV or comic strip supermen. Dell wanted to try but I guess we were all more afraid of getting caught than we were anxious to test out powers.

So we started reading each other's thoughts. It was amazing how accurate we were. I wonder if the foreign substance in our bodies had anything to do with that. After a while we all had to stop and throw up. Then it was gone, all of the excitement as well as the strength. We were just a bunch of bitching young turkey tails, mad about everything and wanting the hell to get home to nice soft warm beds and some decent food.

We drove right past the ski resort turn-off and into a motel just three hours from home. I was bushed and it seemed like such a damned stupid thing to have done, wasted all that meat, drunk gobs of blood, which just made us throw up, and . . . oh shit . . . the whole thing was a bummer. How did I ever get sucked into this weirdo sick kind of thinking. It doesn't have anything to do with mind control and expansion, it was just the old fashioned, superstitious, stupid, childish kind of stupid thing the world hates and suspects about cults, and rightly so. We were just four asshole kids looking for excitement—any kookie, hair-brained thing to explode the boring, boring, boring every-dayness of average life.

FLESH IS CHEAP!
God, what's got into me?

December 8

All 13 of us cut school this afternoon and went up the canyon to Dell's uncle's cabin. We had stashed the blood and things in the cemetery shed on our way home, now we had to sneak them out into our cars. It was unbelievable! Tina coming out with two gallon jars of blood under her coat and trying to look nonchalant. We laughed ourselves silly on the way up. She looked pregnant with the jars and if she had dropped them, people would have thought she was having the bloodiest miscarriage ever. Eight quarts of blood in a person her tiny size? Would wonders never cease? And her still strutting on down the street, looking as robust as ever after the big loss.

I tried to take the whole thing lightly until we had all the drapes drawn in the cabin and rugs and stuff pinned up over every opening that let in the barest amount of light. It was going to be like a club initiation I told myself . . . dumb but not dangerous . . . I didn't know then about Tina's and Mel's intensity, their insistence and seriousness.

I tried to pass when Tina offered the little vial of blood, having thrown it up once made me cringe. But Tina and Mel both had their little black books out, white writing on black paper, and they demanded that each thing had to be done with precision and exactness. Dell and Brad sitting next to me gagged when they took their tastes, but at least it was just a sip this time and not the spurt spurt spurting cupsful of hot stuff directly from the smelly pulsating cow.

Minutes after accepting the offering my eyes began to roll around in my head and a new kind of lightness lifted up my body. I wanted to accuse Tina and Mel of mixing some of their crazy berry or herb concoctions with the blood but the nice easy feeling told me I really didn't care anymore.

After we, through our vibrations, had changed the hands on the clock, levitated some material things, started fires strictly by mental friction, and done a few other little exercises in control, the animal parts were placed before us, and one by one we consecrated and consumed a bit of the part which we wanted to intensify in ourselves, declaring in return dedication for the rest of our existence to the pursuit of greater knowledge about greater things.

When we first got to the cabin Mel had gone out to the pump house and turned on the water and then the heater, now through a hazy mist I saw why. All the blood was dumped into the tub and one by one we were baptized in it, washing the sins and imperfections of our pre-O life away! Our heads were anointed with a few drops of the urine we had milked out of the bull's dingy as he was laying there. Actually it had been just dribbling out, as was his feces, which I remember had amazed me at the time.

After the blood bath the person moved to the shower and was again anointed and cleansed from aroba, or the influences of the outsiders.

What amazes me most of all, as I look back, is that I wasn't repelled by all the ghoulishness, but rather in-

trigued, at least a part of me was intrigued, the other
part was fighting like a scared cat with turpentine up
his ass.

Tina insists that O is against drugs. She says we just
use natural *herbs* to enlighten our minds and intensify
our auwas, but that's a pile of B.S.

I was stoned crackers. I would have to have been to
have taken part in any of that crazy nightmare movie
madness.

After we'd cleaned up every drop of blood from the
bathroom, like slow-motioned zombies, going through
slow-motioned zombie motions, Tina passed us another
'potion.' Again part of me tried to fight her off but I
couldn't! It was like I'd been given sodium pentathol
or something. I couldn't stop myself from saying and
doing things I didn't want to say and do. I couldn't hold
back! I remember feeling like a prisoner of war or
something, that they had taken my will away.

I fought until I literally could fight no longer and fell
weeping to the floor. Instantly I felt my spirit drifting
out of my body. From this stranger outer position, in
midair, close to the ceiling, I watched my body sit
there, perform functions, repeat astramatas. I could not
control it!

I wondered if Brad and Dell's spirits had left their
earthly tabernacles too—if they had I couldn't see them.

It was kind of a nice feeling until I heard the group
begin to chant together. I didn't know what they were
saying, it was new, but I desperately wanted to get back
into my body, control it, protect it, make it behave,
think right, talk right, do right! Stop saying those crazy
things, other world things I didn't understand, didn't
like! I was afraid! Not just kid-scared but desperately,
sickeningly terror strickenly afraid! Again I fought with

all my might to reenter but however I had gotten out would not let me in, something else—someone else— had taken over. MY BODY . . . ME! I wanted to scream, tried to scream, but no audible sound came out. However *my* body was speaking! Saying things I would not have said. Could never have forced myself to say!

> Our Father which art in Hell
> Hallowed be thy name.
> Thy kingdom come, thy will be done
> On earth as it is in Hell
> Give us this day . . .

I could not stand it and left the room, huddling behind the wheel of Toad begging him to help me, bring me back to sanity and reality. Then worried that something I *could control* would happen to my body I went right through the wall and back into the cabin. Each member was dedicating their soul to a strange flickering orange kind of light on a piece of metal in front of the fireplace. It wasn't like fire or a flame, it was like nothing I had seen before, condensed power or something conducting waves . . . anyway Brad, who had never been the school's greatest athlete, or student either for that matter, put his first finger to his temple and said he would dedicate his auwa if he could be the school's top basketball star. I tried desperately to stop him but it was like he couldn't even feel my clutching and clawing.

Next Dell struggled to his feet in a slow-motioned manner. He too put his pointer finger to his right temple. I tried with every bit of power I had to pull it away, but without my body I couldn't! Dell mumbled that if he could have money he too would dedicate his auwa.

I tried to get to the flame, blow it out, smash it out, cover it with my, whatever was left of me, but some unseen black power held me back. Literally and absolutely bound me. My arms and legs were pinioned to my sides.

Defeatedly I began to cry. As I wept I saw some tears running down the face of my body, even though it was still occupied by something else and I could not enter.

After what seemed like an eternity, with everyone committing themselves to whatever evil force pervaded the area I felt a tremendous surge of pain and found that I was once more in my body, which somehow in some way seemed foreign to me. It, without my permission or favor, had dedicated itself to some mysterious black force for—I couldn't remember what—that part had been blacked out. How strange, when I remembered the rest so well. Was I blocking it out myself because I just didn't want to remember? Was anything too vicious and degrading and degenerate for these forces? Vaguely I recalled someone bringing two Great Danes into the house just as Tina and I had been leaving after I had abused her. Were the people and the dogs? . . . They would have done anything! I remember having felt the same feelings there as I felt at the cabin . . . The same strange vibrations . . . The blackness, the smells. I won't, I can't let myself think about it!

December 11

I haven't felt well. I've gone to school and worked my few hours but I simply haven't the energy for anything else. It's like my body's wasted, for good and eternally wasted. Man, if something doesn't happen soon to get me upped I'm going to have to see a doctor or a shrink. The bummer keeps bumping by and by and by!

Each day I feel worse. Tina wants to use her powers to heal me but I won't let her, and I won't use them for myself. I'd rather be sick! She conducted the forum today and seems even brighter and more bubbly than ever—but me . . . old man me, I'm suffering from nightmaritis. Chronic nightmaritis! Did they? Did someone take over my body? Can they do it again?

December 13

This is a miracle. Can one call an O power a miracle? Today Brad, who couldn't make a basket when he had free throws, couldn't miss! He scored twelve points in one game, more than he's scored in the whole season. What a coincidence! Or was it? Dear God, it had to be!

December 14

Brad and Dell and I are like three little kids, lost in the deepest part of the dark and scary woods. We don't want to talk about O and we can't think about anything else. All the chicks in the area plus the coach are treating Brad like an idol, but like he says, the thing he thought would make him the happiest person in the world isn't making him happy.

December 15

Tina came over and sneaked through my window and into bed with me but I couldn't get it on. I didn't even want to. It's like I'm not me anymore. Like I'm two people in one body . . . fighting, struggling for dominance. Oh hell, won't morning ever come? The darkness is my enemy. All evil lurks inside and hides it so I cannot see. But it sees me.

December 18

Things are going from worse to impossible. I'm fighting a losing battle with . . . whatever. Tina and Mel are planning a big anoua for December 24 but *I will not be a part of it!* I told her I wouldn't and she just smiled.

December 19

Brad won another basketball game by thirteen points! He hated it!

December 20

Dell's old aunt in Las Vegas sent his Christmas present early. Can you believe everything she owns to him? Her car, practically new, a $13,000 bank account so he can go to college, plus the old L.V. house clear. In a few years the land alone will be worth a fortune. It's only one block from The Strip. She's had three heart attacks in two days and her doctor says she has no chance at all to recover. Another coincidence? Strange but, I insist, possible!

2:13 A.M.

There is something . . . someone in this room. I can feel it. I can smell it. I cannot see it, only the aura that

emanates from it. It's black and murky yellowish-green.
Oh God, please make it go away.

3:49 A.M.
It's still here. Will it never go away?

December 21

Brad and Dell and I sat up all night and talked. We
declared we had to get ourselves put together. We're
going to chuck O completely! Once and for all! Get
out! It's got us all so screwed-up we don't know reality
from unreality anymore. Brad and Dell have both felt
foul presences in their rooms too, even though we now,
all three, are sleeping with our lights on like little scared
kids.

4 A.M.
Won't it ever get daylight? Won't this thing ever ever
go away? It stands in the corner by my desk and stares
at me. I can't see it completely but I can feel its glare.
Once I reached out to grab it, and saw its hand, just
like mine only of a darker, not so dense, matter, lash
back. I felt nothing, which is strange because I know
it can restrain me! Dell says the beings who sometimes
surround him are always laughing: silently, goadingly,
knowing-something-that-he-doesn't-know, laughing.

> I dare not go to sleep.
> I dare not ask the Lord my soul to keep.
> No matter what the results—*I am out!*

December 22, NITE

Well, I cried today. Tina is going out with some bastard from Fairfax (God, what a hick). Man, sitting talking to her on the phone and my mind so shattered. Oh shit, this is going to be one fucked-up weekend.

Yes, I cried today. It seems so much like the beginning of the end. I would attempt to discourage this beginning but it's her show too. The empty feeling inside is like a silent earthquake, a hush a boom hydrogen bomb. Why oh why does it seem like my whole insides are making the transition from whole to part? She's part of me, I love her. I made the investment of my heart but the love market is down. I'm losing, going down, she kept me afloat but I'm beginning to sink. Why in God's name do I love her . . .

(How ironic, tonight I spent ten dollars on her Christmas present.)

December 23

I just read yesterday's 'everybody feel sorry for me' bullshit and I think it's about time I changed the name of that tune. Man, my ass has been dragging for so long I've almost forgot how to get it off the ground. I've just simply got to pull my head out and start doing something constructive from the inside out. It's like now I'm building from the outside in, and it's not working. I imagine it's something like a carpenter trying to build a house with the roof and the exterior first. It just can't be done! Much as it craps me I guess I've got to start conforming a little more, building on the good old proven things, stop being so afraid I'm going to let somebody else be right, or smart, or have an idea of their own. Anyway, right here—right now—all the never-never land, make-believe, magic, witchcraft bullshit is going to be flushed down the crapper where it belongs. I'm going back to the good old proven dependable, you-can-count-on-it concepts.

Now, today, this minute, is the time to get my life back in order. I've been screwing up long enough. I'm going to get my priorities all straightened out. Nobody controls my mind but me! Nobody is responsible for my half-assed thinking and actions but me! Nobody can set forth general characteristics, interests and goals *for me* except me! So here goes nothing . . . and everything . . .

December 24

DEAR GOD:

How nice to wake and find—
You've given me a brand-new day,
Which I can use in any way.
I lie here in *my* soft warm bed,
My pillow underneath *my* head.
The world is mine. Your gift to me,
THIS DAY IS MINE, and I am free—
Dear God, what will I make it be?
A thing of love, of joy and care?
Something wonderful and fair?
That tonight, as the sun is sinking low
I can, with special inner glow,
All unashamed, and filled with glee
Present more proudly back to thee.
Dear God, this I hope I can do!
For me!—and you.

Christmas Eve

Family, Brad and Dell, life is looking up after all the blackness. Brad and Dell are so understanding about how I feel. They keep telling me I'll get over Tina like I got over Debbie, but that was different. It's like I'm only part of a person without Tina . . . without . . . that's stupid! And I won't let myself think that way— won't let her or anything else control me!

I bought a neat digital watch for Kendall and a turquoise ring for Chad and a catcher's mitt. For mom I bought her favorite perfume which she always says is too expensive and makes her feel like she's being extravagant. I love making her feel extravagant and special. She is special! She is the most special mom in the whole world! And dad, nothing material in life could ever represent in the slightest his worth to me, but anyway I bought him a fishing pole.

And Brad and Dell, we opened our presents tonight in my room. I'm so lucky to have two such wonderful, all through my lifetime, forever after, friends. I'm glad I've got money so I can buy them nice things, not that I'm trying to buy their friendship or their love, just that I'm trying to tell them how important they are in my life . . . in my eternity . . .

Man, I've got a headache! Like someone's in there pounding to get out or someone's out here pounding to get in. Oh Judas, why did I have to think of that? And ruin my whole night.

December 25

Brad and Dell and I went to church together. We partook of the Sacrament and rededicated ourselves to things we understand and, deep down inside, always have believed in and respected.

We were all three sick to our stomachs and headachy and hurting all over but that's probably because we didn't get any sleep last night and we've been eating Christmas goodies and junk for the past few days, or maybe we're coming down with the flu.

Hail the Christ child!

Everybody knows what I'm aiming for. Everybody knows why I'm here.

I'm lookin' for a place to hide and boy I'm gettin near.

The girl that moved me left. I'm here alone, above the clouds, below the rain

It's such a shame I love her. The reasons were simple yes, and no answers to questions of freedom and loneliness. My caress could not find her or bind her

She's gone

Out of the dream of a lasting time

She changed her mind and said that no one knows what she must be. Leave her be.

A ransom of happiness the price to pay

I heard her say. She's gone.

2:43 A.M.

I've never been in a more scary winter storm. Usually I love the snow and the wind, tonight it's lethal.

I wish I thought that I had lost my mind, but I know I have not! The experiences I am living through are real. They are not flashbacks of a drug-sodden mind. Oh Judas, how I wish they were!!!!

About an hour ago I got up because I could feel that

someone was staring at me. I got up and tried to turn on all the lights in the room but they wouldn't work—only the small light that I am afraid to sleep without remained glowing. I flopped onto my knees to pray but the staring entity, with a cosmic-consciousness type of power stopped me.

Breathing heavily I forced myself to look up. Across the bed from me was a person, I swear by all the Bibles in the world! He was real! As real as I am real! His skin was more gray than mine, like more refined matter, where did I hear that? But other than that he is just like me. Probably in his late twenties, good looking, sharp and thin, wearing a gray kind of tight-fitting jump suit thing. Our whole conversation remains seared upon my mind word for word:

'Hello again Jay.'

'Who are you?'

'I'm Raul.'

'What do you want?'

'You know,' he smiled, a most knowing frightening little mouth twist.

'But you're not real.'

'I'm not?'

I pulled away, having to know but not really wanting to ask. 'W . . . Who are you?' I whispered hoarsely.

He folded his arms across his chest and in a mocking way stated matter of factly, 'Remember the third of the host of heaven that were cast out without bodies?'

I nodded weakly, wanting more than anything in the world for the whole thing to be a bad dream but knowing beyond a shadow of a doubt that it was not.

'Wh . . . what do you want?'

He grinned. 'Would you believe . . . your young virile bod?'

I buried my head in the covers, cutting my cheek on the belt buckle I had left on the bed. 'Our father . . . our father . . .' I tried to pray, but it was like mental arm-wrestling, Raul's pressure against mine, and me from the beginning knowing, somewhere in the back of my mind, that *he* would win. He had a wedge in somewhere, like his foot in the doorway of my mind and try as I would I couldn't get it out.

'There's no way I'm going to let you . . .' I mumbled.

He interrupted, 'You already have!'

'No.'

He reached over and ran his fingers through my hair. I cringed.

'Not once,' he hesitated, 'but twice.'

I remembered both times and whimpered, 'But no more! I swear no more!' Raul laughed aloud, 'Want to bet?'

There was something shockingly unreal about Raul talking like just anybody, dressing like just anybody, looking so . . . ordinary and unstrange. Evil spirits . . . devils, looked . . . always in horror movies they looked . . .

'How?' he asked, reading my mind.

I shrugged.

'Feeling more relaxed now you've accepted who I am?' he asked.

I panted, 'I guess so.' But I was cold! All the way through my body frozen cold!

'Not so scared?'

I took a deep breath. 'It's so unreal. . . . I can't believe . . .' My teeth chattered so much I couldn't finish the sentence.

Raul sat down at my desk like he owned it, 'Why?'

'I don't know.'

'You've always known we existed.'

'Yes . . . and no . . . I . . .'

'You mean you didn't want to believe!'

'Maybe.'

Raul looked grim, 'How did you feel when *you* didn't have a body?'

I gritted my teeth, hugged myself and tried to draw my head and arms and legs into myself like a turtle.

'You wanted a body desperately, just like I want one, didn't you?'

I started crying, yelling inwardly for dad to come help me.

Raul got uncomfortable, 'Stop that!'

I blubbered, 'Dad, dad, I want you, need you!'

Raul growled and swung at me. I felt nothing.

Somewhere during our conversation I had heard Hamlet, Kendall's cat, making the ugly weird sounds he makes only when he's in heat or fighting. As the sounds came closer to my room Raul disappeared.

Not wanting to awaken the family, not feeling that I could handle any more at this point, I ran out into the dark hall to get Hamlet and let him out. He hissed, jumped at me, and I could tell from the look in his eyes that Raul had taken over his body.

I wanted to scream, run, jump in bed with my parents, or get the boy scout hatchet and hack the cat into little bits, but what good would that do?

Feeling I was suffocating and being overwhelmed by the stench Raul had left to permeate the house, I ran to the front door.

As Hamlet shot off through the dark, mom, dad, Kendall and Chad all came running down the hall.

'What's that awful smell?' Mom asked.

'If you let that damn cat go stinky in the house again,' Dad threatened.

'It's not *my* cat,' I screamed, relieved at being able to dare scream.

'It smells worse than the time we went past the oil refinery,' Kendall said, holding his nose.

Chad ran over and clung to dad's legs. 'I'm scared. I had a dad bream,' he said, mixing up his letters the way he had when he was very little.

Kendall went closer to mom, 'Me too . . .

Dad put one arm around mom and one around me, 'Strange,' he whispered, 'so did I.'

I could feel mom shaking but she tried to be light, 'Crazy family, having community nightmares. Even Hamlet is screaming out in the lilac hedge.'

She led us all into the kitchen for hot chocolate.

Oh dear God, how I do wish it had all been a nightmare!

I've got to make myself talk to dad about it, but not tonight . . . not tonight . . .

December 29

I was so happy the day after Christmas when we left to go see Aunt Laura in Phoenix. I had wanted to get away! I had to get away from—mainly Raul—and his cohorts—more than I'd ever wanted anything in my life.

Now to come home to this! Brad dead! I still can't believe it! I won't believe it!

Brad was just peacefully driving out of the Blue Moo when the dumb truck turned the corner and, running with its left front wheel on the high curb, crashed over the hood of his car. Dell said the bumper hit him directly on the right *temple* like a giant hammer, killing him instantly. Why there? It's so awful. It's so useless. Such a coincidence. Brad, 16½, barely starting in life.

I didn't even get to pay my last respects or go to his funeral. Maybe that's a good thing. I would have cried like a baby, made an ass out of myself, embarrassed his family . . . Oh God, I wish I knew what happened to him—especially him, after death.

> Cub Scout together, we
> Three
> In kindergarten and
> In grade, and Junior High and High
> How dare you die
> And leave me here
> In fear,
> Of all the great unknown
> Alone.
> You know the answers now,
> No problems, intrigues,
> Stress or strife.
> I miss you so! I loved you so!
> But love you more in death
> Than life.

11:27 P.M.
Dell came over and spent the night. I wonder if anyone else in the whole world knows how we feel? The loneliness, the love . . . the guilt! Oh dear God, we're both so confused. We curled up in each other's arms on my bean bag and cried like we did the time we got stranded on the broken ledge when we were about seven. Bawling, bawling, bawling, no way out until morning came. I remember the howl of coyotes back somewhere in the hills, and the darkness . . . the terrible, awful, consum-

ing, engulfing darkness. That same darkness is with us now, but this time it's like it's inside. Even keeping on the light all night doesn't get rid of it.

Tina told Dell at the funeral that Brad had known he couldn't get out. That no one can get out once they've dedicated themselves. But we were not responsible even if it is real. We were all stoned! Tina and Mel had given us . . . whatever . . . mixed with that blood and . . . oh dear God, it's too awful.

Dell is lying at the foot of my bed in his sleeping bag, slumbering fitfully. Oh God, what have we done with our shining birthrights and heritages?

Before we tried to sleep (he made it, I haven't obviously), I got out my trusty Bible and we took turns reading in the New Testament. It's so beautiful and peaceful. I especially like Matthew, Mark, Luke and John. Dell and Brad and I studied those four books in seminary one semester. How kind and gentle and good those men were. How they loved Jesus and tried to follow his teachings. They cast out evil spirits too. That wasn't unusual in those times. Maybe that's what Dell and I need, and maybe we shouldn't wait too long. Oh Judas, I wish I dared talk to my dad about it. He'd know! I wish I dared go right up in his bedroom now and ask him to come down here and talk to us. He would! But would he, could he understand? I don't want to hurt him anymore. Maybe we should talk to someone else. Our seminary teacher, the Bishop. I'll talk to Dell about it in the morning. It's just a matter of *who* to talk to now, and I feel better.

December 30

I tried to talk to the Bishop, actually made an appointment, then chickened out. When Dad and Uncle John asked Dell and me if we wanted to go cross country skiing with them for the day to try and get our minds off Brad's death, I called and cancelled saying my problem wasn't serious. Actually, I do think things are getting better. Basically, Dell and I just need time to clear our heads, get things together, get back our strength. The shock of Brad's death was too much! But at least it made us see how far off the track we were.

The skiing was fantastic. Powder snow floating out behind us like wings. The sky was so blue and clear it made the pine trees seem an unearthly different shade of green, and when we stopped and dad made a fire and cooked our meal it was . . . Oh Judas, why didn't we have more fun? Why couldn't it have been like old times? Everything's beginning to bug me—school, the folks, forever tending kids. I'll be glad when school starts again. Man, I'm uptight!

Hmmm. It seems as though there are a lot of repetitions of ideas in this here 'book' of mine. They are important so no harm in it.

I'm all alone today with something on my mind.
I'm searching for someone, a person I can't find.
Just thinking back to times, that person I could see
Just wondering if all that time that person could see
  me.

It seems like I should have better things to do than sit around and watch a bunch of shitty kids. The minute I turn my back they screw up and my mind breaks. I get blamed for it.

January 4

How gray the day. One nightmare on top of another.
Bondage . . . psychological bondage! Fear so near
. . . Raul so close.

Mom coming in and saying Dell's Aunt Dicey called
and told her *Dell is dead! First Brad . . . Now Dell
. . .* my heart is warped.

> No, no
> I will not let you go
> Till I go too
> Then we will be
> Again, the three.
> Say Hi, to Brad
> And take him by the hand
> He'll understand
> That soon we'll be
> Again the three

Oh dear God, how can I be so morbid? It's just another of Kendall's coincidences. Mom said, with tears
streaming down her face and overflowing from her soul,
that it was! I know she loved Brad and Dell almost as
much as I did. She baked us cookies and homemade
bread and jam, and special cakes when birthdays came
around. Oh death . . . how sad the sound.

Only last night Dell said that he was going to the
Bishop Sunday. That nothing, absolutely nothing, could
stop him—even me! Then we cried and I promised I
would not try to stop him, but I would help him, encourage him. . . . MAKE HIM GO! Now it's too late!

Of course it was a coincidence!

Larry called and gave me the details. Dell's car
stalled on the Freeway just off the Twenty-third Street

ramp for some dumb reason. He started walking back to Stabley's Gas 'n Go to get Myron or Jake to come help him. Just at the foot of the ramp he got some gravel in his shoe and sat down on the shoulder to shake it out.

A carful of kids from school were pulling off the ramp, not going fast or stoned or drunk or anything, and as they pulled off, Kyle, who was driving, told Larry it was just like someone grabbed the wheel of the car out of his hands and swung it to the right. Larry in the back could see the car swerving directly towards Dell. Kyle started pulling and pulling and the kids started screaming but Dell's head was down and the bumper hit him guess where? *Directly on the right temple* . . . just like Brad! Oh dear God, I can't bear the pain! I can't!

Kyle just phoned. He's so broken up he could hardly talk but he knew how close Dell and I were and he wanted me to hear his side of the story and know how sorry he was. I felt better just sympathizing with him and trying to make him feel better. He's coming over after a while and we're going down together to the mortuary to see Dell's body if they'll let us and where the accident happened and everything. Kyle said he didn't know if he could ever drive his car again, so I'm going to pick him up.

MIDNIGHT

I am soooooo tired! How can emotional shocks make you so physically tired?

They wouldn't let Kyle and me see Dell's body at the mortuary but we went by and saw his folks and cried and talked with them for a while. Man, they're taking it good. They loved him so much, and thought he was such a good kid. I'm glad they don't know. I'm *really glad!*

Kyle told me he didn't think he'd ever sleep again, that he'd always be dreaming he was trying to wrestle his car back onto the road, away from Dell, just innocently sitting there emptying the stones out of his shoe.

Kyle said everyone felt the steering mechanism had malfunctioned but *he knew it hadn't!* Jim Kroller at the garage had checked it over minutely directly afterwards and there was not one damn thing wrong! I wanted like hell to explain to Kyle about Raul and the forces and the third of the hosts and everything, just so he would feel better and less personally guilty, but how could I? I certainly don't want him mixed up in that garbage shit. Maybe in time he can forget and forgive himself. Will I ever be able to?

January 5

Dell in his casket looked like he was asleep. They had turned his head so the right side didn't show. Oh the gruesomeness of it! When I looked at that body I could again see him putting his pointer finger to his right temple and declaring with his life that he would dedicate himself to . . . I can't even write it . . . I went to the men's room and puked and puked and puked, everything I'd eaten for days and then some, and it was red, like blood. Most likely I had broken a little blood vessel in my stomach or throat with my retching, or was it part of the rituals? Part of the mutilation ceremony? Part of the driving me crazy bit? Is that my price to pay? Will institutionalization be my end?

Dear God, will I ever be the same again, or sane? Will I be next? Anyway, *I will not go back on Dell and*

Brad! My external friends. *No matter what I will not!*
Even though Raul and his pack are now really getting
to me. It's becoming harder each day because Raul likes
different music than I do, different food, pornography.
Oh Judas, I hate him so! With a kind of hate I've never
known before.

January 10

Tina is being so kind and friendly to me it's hard to
keep away from her; she brought me chocolate chip
cookies and a batch of fudge. Also a note saying how
badly she felt and vowing her love forever but . . . I
guess I'm going bananas but I really feel that she is
Brad and Dell's enemy, even in death. That's sick—sick
and paranoid and dumb! But it's still the way I feel.

January 13

I can't understand how things can go on in school as
they always have, and at home, and work. How Tina
can race up and down the halls laughing and joking.
How she can preside at student government meetings
and assemblies and be a princess at the games and parties and stuff. It's like nothing had ever happened, like
Brad and Dell's lives made only holes in water that soon
filled up for everybody but me. Like she and the others
don't do the crazy things I know they do, after hours.

11:47 P.M.

Next month we're having another debate in Canada,
man I hope I can get my shit together. Last time it was
so neat, and I've got to prepare for the one in Mexico
in the spring. I've *got* to make that one, but I feel so

low, so draggy. Life must go on! Without Brad and Dell? With Raul? Why?

January 14

Tina and I had lunch together. She said she was really worried about me and tried to get me to start coming to their O meetings again. I said, *no way!* She insists, lots of new fun people are coming in and they've found some wonderfully advanced phenomena meanings that would fascinate me. But I don't want to be fascinated anymore. Tina even promised she'd go with me to see Dr. Peters, the head of the psychiatric department at the university so we could find out who we could present the facts we've already gathered to. She said *that* was the least I could do in Brad and Dell's memory. I don't know, I'm so confused and down.

Then she asked me what in hell *would* make me feel better. Trying to force myself to be light I said, if I could have the lead in the play, 'Barefoot in the Park.' Hell, they've already cast and are into rehearsals.

Tina laughed, pecked me on the cheek, like in the old days, and skipped off down the hall. I wonder if I'll ever feel that way again? Skipping? Laughing? Right now it's like I'm alone and carrying the burdens of the world. Without Brad and Dell's help those burdens are *so heavy!*

January 15

Mr. Jensen, head of the drama department, called tonight and asked me if I'd take over the Robert Redford part in 'Barefoot in the Park.' We were at the dinner table and mom and dad said I turned white as a sheet.

Mr. J. said Ty Turner, who had the part, had had his appendix rupture during the night. My blood ran cold. I could just see Tina and her bunch practicing black witchcraft . . . voodoo . . . mambo . . . on Ty. It was a real principle! It could happen! I'd seen it work! But she'd promised me she'd stay out of black stuff. She'd promised.

Why had she done it? She'd already traded me in on the nose picker from Texburg, who was supposed to be such a big . . . whatever . . . I can't even remember what they call male witches anymore. My mind just isn't working like it used to. Oh, Warlock . . .

January 18

I've been reading in the *World Book* about witchcraft. It says from earliest times people have believed in witches by one name or another. Most people no longer believe in witchcraft. But some primitive persons (primitive persons? Tina says 1 percent of all high school kids!) cling to their belief in evil, mysterious powers. Such persons believe that accidents may be caused by an individual who has these mystic powers. They believe that a person who practices witchcraft calls upon spirits or demons to rise up and hurt his or her enemies.

The *Book of Knowledge* states that formerly people 'thought that the world was divided into a kingdom of good and a kingdom of evil.' It is! Oh, if all human beings would only accept the fact that it is! They would keep themselves from *so much hurt and pain!* Like me . . . I'm lost, in limbo . . . I don't want to go down, and I don't seem to be able to go up. It's so physically and emotionally and spiritually painful. Raul now comes and goes at will, even when I'm around others. Kendall and Chad both can feel him, although they can't see him. I can tell by the look in their eyes when he's around. And Hamlet . . . Hamlet always loved to sleep at the foot of my bed when I'd let him. Now he won't stay in the same room with me, doesn't even like to come to the house when I'm there.

I keep remembering the parable of Christ commanding the evil spirits to leave the man and how they went into the swine. Hamlet knows!

I still haven't worked up the guts to talk to dad or the Bishop, but I'm going to. I AM GOING TO!

January 19

The parents are really leaning on me—mad because I didn't take the 'Barefoot in the Park' part, mad that I chickened out of the last debate, mad I wouldn't turn in my essay, mad that I won't . . . can't . . . go to church, mad that I spend so much time in my room . . .

Mom gave me a list of things to do and I can't force myself to get past the first two. I'm being driven out of my mind, out of my own body!

HOW . . . HOW . . . GOD, HOW CAN I EVER GET BACK?

The list—number three, get hair cut. Get hair . . . on that body that no longer belongs to me . . . cut. There's no one inside!

January 22

Tonight I was so lonely for Dell and Brad. I took Chad for a ride in Toad then stopped at 31-Flavors and bought him a double decker of his favorite pralines and cream ice cream. I needed his love and warmth and companionship and I tried to be light and talk about fun things we'd done in our family in the past. But even he can feel Raul . . . who is more and more often with me . . .

When we got home I invited Chad into my room to sit together with me in my bean chair while we played checkers. He used to love that, but tonight he pulled away and looking me straight in the eyes in his honest innocent little way, he said, 'You're not Jay anymore . . . You don't look like Jay . . . You don't smell like Jay . . . You don't act like *Jay.*' He stared at me intently for a minute and then kind of whimpered, 'Who are you?' Afraid of the tone of his own voice, he ran from the room slamming the door behind him.

Sweet little Chaddy, that was so unlike him, but in his childlike purity and incorruption he knows . . . Chaddy alone knows . . . that I no longer control my own destiny, own my own body, I am no longer captain of my ship, no longer master of my soul.

10:49 P.M.
Tomorrow I must, I WILL call the Bishop. I wish it were not so late and I'd do it tonight.

1977, Year of Our Lord
Dear world, I don't want to get my hair cut, I don't want to tend kids, I don't want to see Tina at school Monday. I don't want to do my biology assignment or English or history or anything. I don't want to be sad or lonely or depressed anymore, and I don't want to eat, drink, eliminate, breathe, talk, sleep, move, feel or love anymore.

Tina, it's not your fault. Mom and Dad, it's not your fault.

I'm not free, I feel ill, and I'm sad and I'm lonely

One last request—all my worldly possessions go to Debbie as my wedding present.

A LETTER FROM JAY'S MOTHER

January 26, 1977

DEAR JANIE,

I have had to write so many letters to Jay's friends and tell them about him. He had girl and boy friends from Chicago to California and from Canada to Las Vegas. Jay had been in science fairs, speech meets, thespian plays, dance contests, essay contests, and on many trips all over the country and to Mexico. Everywhere he went he made friends and it wouldn't be long until he would be corresponding with them.

He was a very intelligent person with an I.Q. of 149. When he was in the eighth grade he won the highest award that is given each year by the Air Force in science. He was planning to go into law or medicine when he graduated from high school. He had been asked to run for student body president in his school for this coming year. He was president of the Debate Club, a National Thespian and won the award in school for not losing any of his debates that he participated in this past year. He was helping the school principal with some of the students who had problems with drugs, etc., and was doing an exceptional job with that. He got to liking a little girl who had a drug problem and had gone with lots of boys and had fallen in love several times. As a result she wanted to marry before school was out and had had problems with her family about this so when

Jay started to liking her the mother and father didn't approve and so she and Jay had problems with her folks. For three months they had one hassle after another about this. We tried to get Jay to go with other girls but he had settled his mind about Tina and then all of a sudden one of Tina's old boyfriends showed up and contacted Tina. Jay found out about it and in four days Jay was dead. One night while we were out Jay took a 22-pistol, put it to his right temple and pulled the trigger. He died instantly. He left a suicide note saying he was tired of all the hassles and didn't want to do anything that living people do. He also said that he was sick, sad and unhappy.

We were very sorry that we didn't know that Jay was so deeply troubled and depressed. We knew he was unhappy about a few things and tried to help him all we could but Jay really masked his feelings to the point that he fooled all of us.

We do feel that Jay had lived a pretty full life in his short 16½ years because he had tremendous abilities and was such an intense person. He was a very deep thinker and was so far ahead in his intelligence that I'm sure he will advance much faster with his heavenly father than he could on this earth. Jay's very best boy friend was killed in a car accident a week to the day before Jay was. Another friend was also in one. I'm sure they are together in heaven and doing good there as they did on the earth.

Well I hope I haven't bored you with this long letter but I wanted you to know a little about him. He was a very choice child on earth and we were so happy to have had him with us for the 16½ years that we did.

A NOTE FROM JAY'S MOTHER'S
SCRATCH PAD

DEAR ANYBODY—NOBODY—EVERYBODY:

How much I wish I could share with you—*with anybody*
all the sober awful truth of Jay's life and death—

We did not know—If we had known could we have
helped him?

Would knowing help you? Heavenly Father let knowing *help* somebody!!!!

Please let Jay not have died in vain!!!!

THE END